Taming the Beast

MUZZLING THE BEAST

TINA DONAHUE

Muzzling the Beast
ISBN # 978-1-83943-823-3
©Copyright Tina Donahue 2018
Cover Art by Posh Gosh ©Copyright September 2018
Interior text design by Claire Siemaszkiewicz
Totally Bound Publishing

Totally Bound Publishing books by Tina Donahue

MUZZLING
THE BEAST

Dedication

To my fellow authors at Naughty Literati.
You do romance so well.

Chapter One

"No, no, no—wait." The were folded his arms over his head, his face anguished.

Constance held back a frustrated sigh and dropped her hands. This was the sixth time she'd backed off this evening. The poor slob couldn't decide what memories he wanted her to remove and which he had to keep. "What's wrong now?"

"Everything." He curled into a fetal position on the treatment table, just about taking up residence in her office at From Crud to Stud, a New Orleans' makeover service for supernatural beings. "Give me a sec."

He'd already eaten up forty-five minutes of her shift with his indecision concerning a mortal babe who'd dumped him. Once she'd found out he was a were, she'd been history, no matter how much he'd tried to stifle his beastly urges. Given his animal lust for her, he'd ached to reminisce about every moment they'd been together, until he'd decided he hated her for the ultimate insult—she'd unfriended him on Facebook. Everyone had a breaking point. That was his and he needed her images excised from his brain until he didn't. Back and forth he'd gone, worse than a tween deciding what to wear to middle school.

Constance was a voodoo priestess, not his mom. "Sweetie, I have other clients. You need to make up your mind."

He tightened his arms. "I. Am. Trying."

"Not hard enough." She wanted to smack him upside his head.

She'd already had a worse day than his. Make that a month. Hell, years. Why kid herself? She'd been dating since she was fourteen but wasn't any closer to a grand romance now than she'd been back then. For thirteen years, she'd slogged through countless hookups and fixups that landed her with guys who were the proverbial frogs rather than princes, none interested in her for the long haul. Three weeks ago had been her Waterloo. Radagar, the warlock she'd been dating on a regular basis, had showed up for their night out with another babe hanging on his arm.

The young woman had grinned and wiggled her fingers at Constance, like they were buddies or something.

Given that he and the girl had been almost welded together, Constance hadn't been in the mood to wiggle back. As the only sane one in the group, she'd had to ask the obvious. "Did you forget this is your and my date night or did you confuse my apartment for being the restaurant where we're supposed to be going?"

He'd laughed. "You're too funny. This is Katka. She just turned nineteen."

And had looked way younger, which had made Constance feel like Methuselah. Why Radagar had seemed happy about that had eluded her. Of course, he'd never been much in the brains department. Being a hunk and competent in bed was all she'd asked from him — with a little fidelity on the side, such as not being with other women when they were together. "Why is she here?"

"I thought we'd liven things up." He'd swatted Katka's butt playfully. "She's the newest member of our team."

As if they'd been coworkers rather than lovers. Since Constance hadn't been up for a threesome or more when even newer members had joined the team, she'd broken up with him on the spot, slammed the door in his shocked face and eaten a tub of Häagen-Daz Belgian Chocolate ice cream for dinner chased by Dove miniatures for dessert. That turned out to be the best date night she'd ever had.

Maybe I should give up on men and switch to… Naw, that wasn't going to happen. She was attracted to the opposite sex, while they couldn't seem to disappoint her enough.

Her intercom buzzed then crackled.

"Ah, can you come up here? Now? Right now? This very second in fact?" Heather, the receptionist and Constance's BFF, sounded more unglued than usual. "Sorry I have to ask, really I am, but please, can you come up here? Please?"

As a good fairy and an empathetic healer, Heather was always super polite and apologetic as hell, yet this seemed beyond serious…like maybe a mortal had stumbled into this place. On the few occasions that had happened, Heather had had strict instructions — call Constance to take care of the problem. If the dude or dudine left with memories that involved weres howling and vamps hissing, everyone who worked here was toast.

She spoke into the intercom. "Be right there."

"Thank you." Heather panted. "I mean, really, I am so grateful you're—"

"You bet." She hurried to her office door.

"Hey." The were pushed to a sitting position on the padded table. "What about me?"

She'd forgotten his turmoil. "Hold still."

"What—no—wait."

Constance couldn't. She gripped his head and did the only thing she could. She removed his memories of her.

He blinked then frowned. "Who are you?"

"The site medic. You fainted during treatment."

He gripped her wrist and regarded her shadowed, sensuous office. Wispy smoke rose from incense sticks on her desk. Candlelight glinted off beaded curtains and created colorful dots on the ceiling and walls. "How'd I get in here?"

"Couple of the enforcers carried you in from the other room. Don't you dare leave until I get back to make sure you're okay."

He spied her laptop. "While you're gone, do you mind if I use your computer to get on Facebook? There's something I have to check out."

Of course, he did. Poor thing hoped his ladylove had friended him again, and if she hadn't, he could leave a nasty message using Constance's ISP address. "Be my guest."

The intercom buzzed. "Are you coming? Please?"

"Yeah, right away." Constance pointed her bejeweled finger at him. "Hang tight."

She raced down the hall and stopped short before reaching the reception area. Its coral walls, gas light fixtures, faux brick floor, numerous potted plants and feathery ferns created an earthy and romantic feel, which screamed mortal to fool the unsuspecting who happened inside.

This one must be pure awful. Heather stood behind her chair, possibly for protection, digging her nails into the leather, her face ashier than usual. Its tint matched her pale blonde hair and signature white clothing.

Constance edged around the corner, leery and curious as to whoever had scared the bejeezus out of Heather.

The guy faced Constance, but his gaze was on the ceiling. Thankfully, no vamp had morphed into a bat and was buzzing around up there.

Despite the steamy summer night, he wore a blue suit, white shirt and gray tie, the clothes draping him beautifully. Deliciously tall, he had to be six three or better, broad in the shoulders, his hips narrow, his build lean yet muscular.

Warmth filled her when it shouldn't have. Radagar's stupid stunt had cured her of men for a long, long time. Then again… She clutched her full-length gown since it wouldn't be polite to grab this guy. What a hottie. He wore his curly black hair cropped short. His cinnamon-colored skin was a stunning contrast to his light blue eyes, his features masculine and a trifle rough.

Her pulse quickened.

She guessed him to be Creole, early thirties, an executive and probably mortal given Heather's reaction. Most women would have been drooling by now, not hyperventilating. In another few seconds, she might be out cold and Constance would have to give her CPR. She would have preferred to do that for him.

To break the ice, she inched closer. "Well, hey, there."

He took her in from stem to stern, his attention snagging on her saffron-colored turban and matching gown then lingering on her mouth and boobs. Like he couldn't help himself.

She wasn't about to complain. Call her crazy, but the lovely bulge behind his fly seemed to thicken in interest.

Her pussy creamed in response.

Heather wasn't as taken. With him turned away from her, she waved her arms in what looked like warning.

Constance couldn't imagine why. For her to cup his good-looking head and remove his memories of this place would be more play than work.

He met her gaze. "Evening."

His rumbling baritone registered clear to her tongue and tonsils. She smiled.

Male interest sparkled in his gorgeous eyes. He killed his arousal and got ultra-serious. "I'm Detective Gabe Legrand."

Constance's heart stuttered. He couldn't mean as in a freaking cop but probably did. Her smile went kaput over what had brought him here. Not to mention what would happen if others in his department suspected something weird was going on within these walls. "You're with the police?"

He lifted a small leather wallet that displayed a silver shield, its crescent engraved with a word, maybe *detective*. The thing was too far away for her to read. Beneath the crescent was a star with another word and a number.

She wouldn't have been surprised if it was 007, considering his awesome looks.

He pocketed his badge and advanced with stunning grace, similar to an animal in the wild stalking its prey. God help her, she was still more tempted than alarmed and drifted toward him in what seemed like slow motion. Another step and they'd touch. She didn't see the harm.

He stopped. "You're the owner?"

Heather made a pained sound. "Constance is a good person."

Not that good. His woodsy-musky scent warmed her as the sun never had and made her legs watery.

"Your name is Constance?"

"Guilty as charged." She hoped a joke would lighten the moment so Heather wouldn't faint or blurt the truth about this place since good fairies couldn't lie. "Nice to meet you, Detective. Or can I call you Gabe?" She offered her hand.

His own was so large it swallowed hers, his palm dry and slightly callused, his grip firm but not intimidating.

Heaven in a handshake. She liked a man who took charge, in particular when it came to bedroom play. Not that a roll between the sheets seemed possible, given his slight frown.

"I thought Becca Salt owned this place." He spoke to Heather. "Didn't I ask you to call the owner up here?"

Heather gripped her chair so hard her knuckles got even whiter. "Uh-huh."

"Then why didn't you?"

She clenched her jaw.

Before she broke her molars, Constance jumped in. "She did. I'm the owner. Constance Salt."

Gabe regarded with suspicion, though his attention did wander to her mouth, boobs and her hand as she released his. "Then who's Becca Salt? The name listed on the permits and other papers as the owner."

"Still me." Constance leaned toward him as if to share a big, bad secret. "My first name's Becca, but I hate it, so I go by my middle name with coworkers and friends." She gave him a sweet smile and gestured to the hall. "Why don't we go to my office to talk?"

Rather than follow her, he glanced past.

Becca strolled toward them. Her silky blue halter-top and harem pants shimmered beneath the lights, as did her jewelry. Silver stars dangled from her navel, dainty chains decorated one ankle and rings glittered on her toes. Coupled with her flame-red hair, alabaster skin and the heavy Goth makeup she wore around her eyes, she was one of a kind. Not to mention a witch, in the literal not figurative sense.

"Lorraine." Constance glared at Becca. "What are you doing roaming around? Have you finished the accounts? You need to do those payables tonight."

Becca halted, took in the scene and lingered on Gabe. She got paler than Heather, most likely because she figured something was way wrong. "Uh, sorry. Won't happen again." She pivoted and hurried away.

"Whoa. Wait. You're going in the wrong direction." Constance pointed to her own office. "Do your work in your spot, not mine."

With the were still inside her space, Constance couldn't bring Gabe in there.

"Right." Becca offered a sheepish smile and raced toward Constance's office.

Gabe's face masked whatever he thought. "She's your accountant?"

"A nice person generally, but... Let's face it, good help is so hard to find these days. Follow me."

A were, maybe hers, let out an ear-piercing howl. The vamps chorused their hisses. Demons' growls and grunts joined in.

Eyes wide, Gabe shoved his hand inside his jacket.

Constance would have bet he was reaching for his gun, not his badge.

He turned from side to side, neck craned, gaze searching. "What in the hell's going on here?"

"Therapy."

"What?"

She affected her most professional demeanor. "That's all I can say. It's all I will say even if you have a warrant. There is such a thing as shrink-client confidentiality, you know."

The were bellowed.

Gabe kept his hand inside his jacket. "Shrink? That's what you call your so-called therapists?"

Talk about hurtful. "I'm as laid-back as they come." Constance ran a tapered nail over her jawline. She liked his stubble and wanted to stroke it. "No need to use big words, now is there?"

"Exactly what kind of therapy do you do here?"

"The usual."

"Meaning?"

"Let's discuss it in my office." She gestured to Becca's.

He stayed where he was. "Why not here?"

She wanted to be alone with him. Odd. Mortals had never appealed to her, which made him uber special. "Because." It was the only answer she could come up with. He'd fried her brain with his scent, occupation and great looks.

He eyed her skeptically. "Because of what?"

Time to get tough, or as much as she could with an Adonis like him. "Ah...confidentiality. Only staff and clients are allowed in the reception area. Since you're neither, and our clients aren't expecting a stranger, you'll have to follow me."

He trailed far behind her.

Didn't matter. They'd end up in the same spot together. Her blood thickened, though not for long. Once they were alone, she'd have to remove his memories to make certain he left forever. The reality distressed Constance and made her chest ache, but she had the business and her coworker friends to protect.

In addition to Heather and her, Becca also employed several demons, a genie and a former satyr. Stuff mortals would never understand.

Once inside Becca's office, Constance panicked at her error in bringing him here. Although there were abundant plants and antique furniture that would have impressed an affluent mortal, there were also numerous pictures of Becca and Eric, her one and only love, on the cabinet.

She'd forgotten about them.

Gabe stepped inside.

She closed the door and blocked him so he wouldn't sit on the sofa and notice the photographs then wonder or demand why she had shots of Eric and Becca in her supposed office.

He backed up.

Constance advanced.

Gabe stopped, not giving any ground.

She enjoyed his style. "So, why are you here, Gabe, or should I call you Detective?"

Lust darted across his chiseled features along with too much wariness. "Can we be honest with each other?"

That wouldn't have been her first, second or last choice unless they were dating exclusively, which was never going to happen. "I don't know what you mean."

"I think you do. Your driver's license, or rather Becca Salt's license, doesn't do you justice. In fact, it shows a white woman with red hair and blue eyes. Exactly like your accountant Lorraine."

Sweat broke out on Constance's neck. She played dumb. "You're here to talk about my license? The Office of Motor Vehicles mixed me up with Lorraine?"

He stepped closer. She didn't give an inch either. They were wonderfully near, allowing her to indulge in the light brown flecks around his pupils. His fragrance surrounded her. She weakened. Damn, she yearned.

Months had passed since she'd been this aroused by a man. Radagar had been cute but too much of a Lothario and a dimwit. The others she'd known hadn't been any better, taking what they wanted, leaving her heartbroken and lonely.

Gabe might prove the same, but his heat and big body still called to everything female within her.

He grew distracted then intense, possibly from the same carnal hunger she felt.

Time seemed to stop.

His breathing picked up.

So did hers.

Someone slammed into the wall behind them, grunted and swore, killing the magic.

Gabe looked past her and frowned. "What is going on here? And don't you dare tell me regular therapy. The business license is for a behavior adjustment and grooming service, whatever that's supposed to be."

"We like to think of it as a finishing school for guys." She smiled. "So many of you are rough around the edges. Wouldn't you agree?"

He gave her a cop's hard stare.

Her pussy got even wetter. She wondered if he liked using his handcuffs during bed play. If there was a God and She was female, Gabe did. "We're simply trying to help guys suppress their uncivilized urges, like women have always been taught to do." She stroked his forearm.

His Adam's apple bobbed from his hard swallow. "That's not what I've heard."

She went hot, cold and hot again, terrified at what he meant. A client couldn't have lodged a complaint with the cops and told the authorities there were vamps, weres, reapers and other paranormal beings here trying to suppress their beasts. It would be lunacy for them to expose their true natures to a mortal.

That only left the police department infiltrating this place with a supernatural who worked undercover, egged on by the Religious Right that saw conspiracies everywhere, even in Barbie dolls and McDonald's Happy Meals.

She was afraid to know the truth but had to. "What have you heard?"

Gabe took in the sofa, the plants and glanced at the cabinet.

Before he got a good look at the photos, she cupped his head and turned his face to hers.

His eyes widened but he didn't pull away. "What are you doing?"

What she shouldn't, wanting him. His tight curls were a major distraction, the same as his rich mouth. She couldn't breathe. "Nothing."

She vaporized his memories concerning why he'd come here.

He blinked and looked at her questioningly.

What could she say, except sorry? She was for having played with his mind, but not for stroking his scalp.

His face went slack. He regarded her features and became lost in them.

Constance drank his in too, liking his looks. She felt comfortable with him, even though they didn't know each other and never would. Sorrow hit deep in her stomach. Beneath the pain she longed for a good man. Someone she could count on who'd make each day a pleasure.

Wasn't going to happen with him. They only had these moments. Her sadness returned. "You okay?"

He stared at her eyes and mouth. "Shouldn't I be?"

As far as his memories were concerned, no. When it came to her touching him, she would have liked him to offer a resounding yes. "Absolutely. You're good...way more than..."

Gabe edged closer, as a man does when he can't help himself.

She couldn't, either. Acting on pure instinct, she guided his mouth to hers.

His lips were heated and super soft, his beard-roughened cheeks a wonder against her smoother skin, so virile and welcomed. She reeled. Sagged against him, she opened her mouth to his, inviting his tongue inside.

He stilled then went full throttle, pulling her against his rock-hard erection and cupping her ass.

She surrendered as she never had and angled her head to offer him better penetration.

Groaning, he speared his tongue more deeply into her mouth, filling it and thrilling her. He tasted like peppermint and a flavor that belonged to him alone. Clean and enticing.

So much so, she couldn't bear removing his memories of her. She wreathed her arms around his neck and dove in for more.

She was pure sin in his arms, her abundant curves snuggled against him, her scent a sultry and spicy combination with deep floral scents.

Gabe wanted to growl like a maniac or whatever slammed into the wall. He hadn't a clue what was going on unless this was the mother of all wet dreams while he was awake.

The last thing he recalled was being on an investigation. Funny thing though, he couldn't remember what the probe entailed. He'd gone blank for a moment, like a computer being rebooted. When he'd become aware again, he'd been staring at then kissing Constance.

Whoever Constance was.

Somehow, details didn't matter. She was so warm, soft and willing in his arms he didn't want this moment to end.

She tried to slip her tongue into his mouth.

He wouldn't allow it. This show was his to run. He deepened his kiss.

She yielded but didn't play dead, her response beyond wanton and sensual, celebrating life and unrestrained need. Stuff Gabe had never engaged in with a woman he didn't know. His disciplined nature had always restrained his lust, even in high school, and especially when it contradicted good sense.

That was then. This was now.

He tightened his arm around Constance's waist and tugged at her turban, needing to know what was beneath it. The headdress fell to the floor. Her hair spilled out. Not clipped short as he'd expected, but long, silky tresses that tumbled halfway down her back.

Even his teeth tingled. She was something — young, beautiful and black, her eyes as dark as midnight, her shape similar to a damn fertility goddess.

It was fucking Christmas in July and she was his gift, unlike any other woman he'd ever met. And he'd known a lot, both good and bad.

He practically devoured her. Constance's pebbled nipples poked him as she strained to breathe. His lungs also burned for air. He pulled his mouth free but forgot to inhale.

The room was unfamiliar. He couldn't recall how they'd gotten inside or why he was here. Misgiving flared in him as to what the fuck was going on.

She lowered her arms and eased away.

Her plush mouth was wet from their kiss and slightly swollen from his passion. Gabe figured he should apologize but was too dumbfounded to speak.

She smiled seductively and ran her thumb over his bottom lip. "Still doing okay?"

Beneath her lusty demeanor, he sensed her concern, which stoked his. "Why wouldn't I be?"

Something crossed her face he couldn't quite interpret.

She dismissed the emotion with a shrug. "No reason. From what I can see, you're young, strong and healthy." She leaned closer. "Very healthy."

Laughter rose in his throat. He pushed it down. "Thanks. Can I ask you something?"

She eased back and wound a tress around her finger.

He wanted to bury his face in her mane and wallow in her wondrous scent.

"Sure." Her playfulness receded. "Shoot."

Although he was reluctant to go on, he didn't have a choice except to ask the dumbest question ever. "How'd we get in this office?"

She eased her hair behind her ear. "You followed me, of course. We were talking and laughing then I attacked you. Sorry." Her grin was frisky rather than apologetic.

Gabe saw no reason to bitch about that. He wore her scent and figured she wore his. Their kiss wasn't something he'd soon forget. "What were we talking about when we came in here?"

She cleared her throat. "Our kiss was so good you forgot?"

Didn't seem possible, but he didn't have a better explanation. "Seems like it."

She laughed gently and stroked his tie. "You were looking for the new nightspot, After Dark. You can see it from the window in here. I was going to show you." She gestured to the right.

He didn't bother to check it out, preferring to drink her in instead.

Constance beamed. The way a woman does when she appreciates a man's full interest.

How could any normal guy afford her less?

"Are you good, Gabe...or do you still need directions?"

"No, I'm set." He was also horny and confused, struggling to recall how they'd come to this point. The memory eluded him. Dismayed, he hoped she could fill him in later while they enjoyed the evening together. "Are you working?"

"You mean employed?"

"Yes. No. That is, yes. I mean, are you working right now?" He glanced around the room and snagged on pictures of a red-headed woman and a guy on the cabinet. Both white and unknown to him. "Do you work here?" Wherever here was.

"I do...why?

Her unease surprised him. He wasn't certain if it concerned something about herself or the weird way he was acting. "When do you get off tonight?"

She stopped stroking his tie. Pleasure then sadness flitted across her face. "Not until dawn."

The odd hours caught him off-guard. This wasn't a hospital or an emergency room. At least, he didn't think so. "What about tomorrow?"

She slumped. "The same. I work nights every single day."

"No time off to ever go out and have some fun?" He chuckled self-consciously. "With me, of course."

Desire filled her gaze. "Ah… No, sorry, I don't have any free time."

He had trouble hiding his confusion. Never had a woman turned him down for a date when she'd shown him such powerful and unguarded interest as Constance had. Before his disappointment defeated him or he felt more foolish than he already did, he lifted his shoulders. "Guess I better get going." He didn't budge.

Neither did she.

Something electric and exciting passed between them that damn near forced him to his knees. He wanted Constance to kiss him again. Hell, he needed to do so with her. Cuddling would have been nice, too, getting to know her the absolute best.

She stepped past him. "I'll show you to the door."

So much for his fantasies. On their way, a chilling howl broke out, similar to a wolf's.

He stopped and cringed at the weird sound.

Hisses followed. Those seemed to come from a huge cat or a snake.

Constance sauntered yards ahead, not alarmed in the least.

Possibly because she was used to noises one would hear in an animal hospital that had round-the-clock service. Unless, she hadn't heard anything. He wasn't certain he had, either. Maybe he was hallucinating for reasons he didn't understand.

Sweating, he reached the front. The young woman at the desk was so white it almost hurt to look at her without sunglasses.

The second she spotted him, she turned her chair around so he couldn't see her.

He hoped he hadn't said something offensive when he first came in. He would have asked but was afraid that might cause her to meltdown worse than he was. The reception area didn't look the least bit familiar. He might as well have been seeing it for the first time.

Didn't make sense. He had to have come through here to get to that office.

"Nice meeting you." Constance offered her hand.

Jeweled rings covered each finger. Despite his misgivings about everything else, he had to smile at her gems and silky gown, liking both. He fantasized what was beneath the dark yellow fabric — flawless ebony skin, dusky nipples, delicate hair between her legs.

He caressed her hand. Her heat and nearness stole his breath. He trembled from intolerable need, desperate to see her again. Maybe she'd shot him down because she had a boyfriend or a husband. Possibly several ex-spouses too, given the numerous rings she wore.

Not wanting to act like a cop and interrogate her, Gabe released her hand. "Same here."

He forced himself to go out to the landing and closed the door. The air was so steamy and thick he found it difficult to breathe.

A guy hung over the wrought-iron railing as if he was going to hurl on the ferns hanging beneath it.

Gabe stepped closer. "Hey, buddy, you all right?"

The guy looked at him.

He tried not to stare but couldn't stop, never having seen anyone hairier and getting more so by the second. Not only was the guy's beard growing heavier, his eyebrows were too, covering half his forehead. No, every part now. Even his throat and hands sprouted the stuff.

Shocked, Gabe backed up.

The guy snarled. "Fucking full moon."

24

Gabe's throat was too tight for him to form words.

The guy huffed out a sigh. "Great. You're mortal. I should've known. Constance!"

She sped to the landing faster than Gabe could blink.

The guy spoke to her. "I tried to fight my urges like Zoe warned, but as you can see, I can't." His teeth elongated like a dog's or a wolf's, the same as his face. Bones cracked and popped. His skin made stretching noises. "The friggin treatment's not working, and this dude's mortal."

She pushed the guy into the office and cupped Gabe's head.

He went blank. When his mind powered back on, he and Constance stared at each other.

She pointed to the right. "After Dark is there. See?"

Without looking, he nodded, confused as to why he'd stopped on the landing since they'd already discussed this inside. He also recalled leaving the front office without her accompanying him.

"Have a good night." She looked at him longingly then raced into the building.

He followed her to the door.

Metal clacked against metal. The sound a deadbolt makes.

Her locking him out.

Chapter Two

Heather buried her face in her hands. "This is all my fault."

She, Zoe and MJ had crowded into Becca's office. Constance slouched on the needlepoint sofa, bummed by what hadn't happened with Gabe. Or rather what could never happen. Even though he'd wanted to go out with her badly, more so than any other guy she'd known, no way could she date him. Their diametrically opposed worlds would collide. He was a mortal cop sworn to keep New Orleans safe and sane, while she was a voodoo priestess helping supernatural predators tone down for mortal babes.

She muttered an oath.

Heather clasped her fists to her chest. "I'm so sorry."

"You didn't cause this." Becca rubbed Heather's back. "It doesn't happen often, but sometimes humans do wander inside."

Zoe stopped pacing. As manager of the enforcing staff, she'd taken to dressing like an executive, her linen pantsuit and heels elegant and feminine. However, she hadn't mellowed all that much since falling in love with three demons who'd come from Hell, as she had. Flames bobbed in her eyes. Her dark hair and shoulders still smoked whenever she was upset.

She batted away the sulfurous vapor. "This sucks." Despite her five-foot-nothing height, her voice was octaves lower than James Earl Jones. Purely demonic.

Becca looked over. "Try to relax and the smoke will go away."

"That's not what I meant. Maybe we should start locking the front door."

"Uh-uh. If weres arrive during a full moon, they have to get inside fast before a mortal sees their transformation."

No way was Constance going to mention what Gabe had seen before she'd obliterated those images from his mind.

"Then there are the vamps." MJ, aka Mistress Jin, plopped on a chair. The bells around her wrists and ankles tinkled. Built better than a Victoria's Secret model, she had gorgeous features, a caramel-colored complexion, violet eyes and long black hair. She was into guys big time whether they were immortal, mortal or otherwise. They couldn't get enough of her, either. She was dating most of the supernatural world and was Daemon and Heather's houseguest, Daemon being Heather's one-and-only love. More than a year ago, he'd come here for a makeover to change from looking like a satyr, his natural state, to human form so he could boogie with mortal babes. He'd ended up falling for Heather instead and now worked here as an enforcer. Before his transformation, MJ had been his genie and lived in his ring until he'd freed her. Since then, she also became an employee and granted wishes to clients for a reasonable fee.

Stuff Constance knew mortals would never understand.

Becca spoke to MJ. "You're right. The vamps could start draining the tourists and locals dry if they can't get in here right away for treatment. It's settled. The door stays unlocked."

Heather made a wounded kitten noise.

"Everything's cool." Becca patted her shoulder. "As long as Constance is here to remove a mortal's memories of this place, we're okay." She looked at her. "You did take out all the detective's recollections, right?"

Guilt slammed into Constance. Rather than answering, she gathered her hair into a loose ponytail and shoved it beneath her turban.

Becca approached, her features tense with concern. "Right? Wait—why weren't you wearing your headdress?"

Zoe's hair and shoulders belched smoke. "She's never taken it off before. I figured it was because she was bald."

"Zoe." Heather gave her a scolding look. "Be nice."

"Hey, I'm being honest, not cruel." She stared at Constance. "What happened between you and him?"

Everything and nothing, which left her frustrated, melancholy and alone, as usual. Worse, Becca and the others were behaving like a tribunal from the Inquisition. Constance loved these ladies, they were her forever friends, but she wanted to smack each on the head for asking too many questions. "He doesn't remember why he came here. I made sure of it. Twice."

Becca sank to the sofa. "Why twice?"

She cursed her big mouth. "Before he left, he saw a were transform on the landing." She spoke to Zoe. "The client mentioned you specifically. Said his treatment hadn't worked."

Zoe lifted her chin. "I handled things."

The poor guy was howling away even now.

Becca took in Zoe and Constance. "So everything's good?"

She had to be kidding. Gabe was beautiful, employed, had a great personality and from what she felt while kissing him, he was hung like the proverbial horse. He was also interested in her, not nineteen-year-old babes like other guys were, and she'd had to let him go.

She covered her eyes.

"Hey, hey." Becca slung her arm around Constance's shoulders. "What's the matter? Did he threaten you? Oh, my God." She sucked in a breath. "Is your headdress off because he attacked you?"

"Seriously? I kissed him first." Constance figured she should be ashamed for being so needy but the feeling didn't come. Yearning did. "I had to. I knew it would be the last time I saw him."

Becca exchanged a glance with the others. "You actually kissed him?"

Zoe curled her upper lip. "A mortal?"

"A. Good-looking. Man." Constance drooped. "I couldn't help myself."

No one commented.

For some reason, that pissed her off more than having to give Gabe up. "None of you get it, do you?"

Becca embraced her. "Get what?"

"The obvious." She rubbed her forehead. "You guys are so used to having someone, you don't have a clue what I go through every time I'm here."

MJ sat up. "At work?"

"What else? Look, I know you have your needs, especially since you were cooped up in that ring for so long, but every single time I walk in on you and a client, you two are lip-locked and tearing at each other's clothes. Call me crazy, but I don't think that's part of the service. When you and Heather are together, you're giggling about or modeling fetish stuff you plan to wear to clubs where there are even more guys." She spoke to Heather. "Whenever I go to your desk, you're pushing food in Daemon's mouth and letting him suck your fingers clean, after which he shoves his tongue halfway down your throat for a fifteen-to-twenty-minute kiss."

Heather went into a full-body blush. "He's always hungry. He's a big guy. He's affectionate."

No way could anyone dispute that given how he was always going at it with her. He was also hung almost as well as Constance suspected Gabe was.

Zoe gave Heather a sour look. "It is disgusting watching you and Daemon get all icky with each other. You guys need to tone it down."

"Are you kidding?" Constance pointed at Zoe. "I'm not one to complain and haven't, but no one eats in the break room anymore since you and the Unholy Trio decided to make it your spare bedroom."

The flames in Zoe's eyes flared, hiding her dark irises. "Can I help it if Stefin, Anatol and Taro are hot-blooded? They're demons, not choirboys. They want what they want when they want it."

"Hon, that only works for two-year-olds. Your guys are what? Into their first or second centuries?"

Zoe tapped her foot. "They're all in their prime. There's nothing wrong with them."

Except they made Casanova look like a damn eunuch. "I'm not saying there is. Hey, you're luckier than I'll ever be. I can't even get one guy, much less three, to attack me in my office or the break room, at least without another woman being present for the fun."

Everyone looked at each other. MJ spoke first. "I didn't know you were into ménages. How about orgies? Ever try them?"

"MJ." Heather shook her head.

Becca squeezed Constance's shoulder. "Are you into—"

"Absolutely not. Radagar brought a little friend along on our last date without my permission. That's what I was referring to. She was presumably of age and very friendly."

"Ew." Becca made a face. "I hope you gave him hell."

"Made him find his way back to his wheels all by himself. Given his IQ, it took him a while."

Everyone laughed, even Heather.

Constance didn't. "I also downed enough ice cream to put me into a sugar coma and push me into a higher dress size."

Becca made a sympathetic sound. "Things will get better."

She'd heard that sorry crap before but didn't bother to ask when or with whom because her newfound luck wouldn't include Gabe. "Do you remember the impact Eric had on you when you first met him?"

"We all do." Zoe pinched her nose. "Becca was pure misery to live with. So what if he was a Roman god and she was a crappy witch, that didn't mean—"

"Hold it." Becca clenched her jaw. "Crappy witch?"

Embarrassment flooded Zoe's pretty features. "Sorry. Half-witch. I keep forgetting about your dad being mortal."

Becca scowled. "Despite my DNA, my spells and potions are starting to work."

Maybe thirty-five percent of the time on a good day. There weren't many of those.

No one mentioned that detail or confirmed her pitiful statement.

"I'm getting better at them. I'm studying hard." She crossed her arms. "Let's not forget this is about Constance, not me."

Everyone's attention shot back to her.

Precisely what she didn't need. "I'm not complaining. I'm happy you guys got your men, love and forever after. I'd just like a little for myself. Sometimes it's hard to spend my nights and days alone or go to award ceremonies where you guys have dates, some have several, and mine stand me up like the last time." She lowered her face to hide her sadness. "Is it a crime for me to want to be with somebody too?"

"No." They'd spoken as one.

Becca cupped Constance's chin. "We want you to hook up with a great guy, really."

"I know. But not Gabe, right?"

"He's mortal." Becca lowered her hand. "We're with other supernaturals."

"Except for MJ. She goes either way."

"Guilty as charged. However, the mortals I hook up with are way off premises." She tucked her feet beneath her, quieting her bells. "If I were to settle down, which I'm not about to, I'd choose an immortal. Makes things easier."

"For you." Constance dropped against the stiff cushion. "Our clients have never been interested in me. Why do you think I have to come on so strong with them, even the ones who aren't my type? If I waited for those jerks to make a move, I'd never see any action." She spoke to Zoe. "Remember when you asked me not to flirt with your guys because you were worried they might not want you? Well, sweetie, the way you felt then is the way I am all the freaking time."

Zoe's hair stopped smoking. She knelt at Constance's side and rubbed her knee. "I had no idea. You're so gorgeous I thought every man who met you fell head over heels."

Heather stroked Constance's turban. "Me, too."

"Same here." MJ left her chair and squeezed Constance's shoulder.

They loved her and it was nice, but not enough after meeting a guy like Gabe. She wasn't naïve enough to believe he didn't have any crappy habits. Maybe he whistled off-key, watched too many sports and failed to take out the garbage.

No one was perfect, though to her he was damn close. He'd made her feel desired and special. Losing that caused her heart to sink.

Becca regarded Constance. "Did he say what had brought him here?"

"He danced around it. All he admitted to was that he'd heard things. Unless he was lying about that."

Color drained from Becca's face. "Heard things? Like what?"

"I have no idea."

Becca shot a worried look at the others. "You guys never talk shop with mortals, right?"

They offered a collective gasp. The same response one would expect from an elderly nun who'd been questioned about masturbating during confession.

Zoe batted away new smoke. "Are the permits in order?"

Becca and the others looked at Heather.

She backed away from their questioning gazes. "I filed everything exactly as I'm supposed to and paid the fees. I even overpaid the IRS from my own checking account so they wouldn't cause us any problems."

MJ shook her head. "Keep it up, sweetie, and you'll go broke."

"So? I don't want anything bad happening to this place."

Becca took Constance's hand. "Tell us exactly what he said. Don't leave anything out."

She shared everything, except for her and Gabe's deep, lingering kiss and how he'd made her want what she'd never have.

Becca bit her lower lip. "Maybe someone made a complaint about the noise."

The weres, demons and vamps were going at it tonight, the way POWs do when torturers yank out their fingernails and teeth. The treatments here weren't a day at the beach but they weren't that bad.

Becca spoke to Zoe. "You better keep the racket down."

"Sure thing." She smacked her fist into her palm. "I'll have my guys take care of it immediately."

"Hold on. No broken bones, bruises or blood flying. I don't want Heather leaving the reception area to heal anyone."

"You're sure? The extra fee brings in big bucks."

"There are more important things to consider now. We need her to keep an eye on the front door."

MJ sat on the sofa arm. "Say the word and I'll fix this so we never have another problem."

"Seriously?" Concern filled Heather's green-gray eyes. "No fooling around?"

In the past, MJ had granted wishes so literally the recipients had regretted what they'd asked for. Like Daemon when he'd wanted his satyr tail, hooves and horns to go away. MJ had sent his legs running without him attached to them. After that fiasco, he'd come there for a professional makeover.

Becca stopped chewing her thumb. "Fix it in what way?"

"By installing security cameras and soundproofing the rooms."

"Great idea. Put one camera outside to show who's coming up the stairs and to the door then soundproof the rooms, nothing else. No making the neighbors or tourists go deaf so they can't hear anything. Heather told me what you did at her place so Daemon's heavy metal wouldn't bother anyone."

MJ shot Heather a look.

She pretended not to notice.

"You don't have to worry." MJ's mouth turned down. "No matter what, I'll be good."

"I appreciate that." Becca pushed her bangs off her forehead. "We'll make this place quiet as a tomb, just in case the noise brought him here."

Zoe made a face. "Do cops usually check out stuff like that?"

"Maybe not regular ones." Heather clasped her hands. "His badge showed he's a detective."

"Like those dudes on *Law and Order SUV*?"

"That's a vehicle." MJ arched one eyebrow. "I believe you mean SVU. Great show, by the way."

"Whatever." Zoe gestured dismissively. "Detectives fight serious crimes. So why would he come here over a simple noise complaint?"

Becca spoke to Constance. "You're absolutely certain you removed all his memories of the business and his investigation, if there is one?"

Constance's throat tightened from sorrow. "Yeah."

Becca didn't look convinced. "I know how lonely you are. I've felt exactly the same in the past. But you have to understand, supernaturals depend on us. If we weren't here, where would they go to suppress their beasts?" She gripped Constance's shoulder. "We're your family, like you'll always be ours. We need to protect each other. So please tell me when you removed his memories of the business, you also took out the ones involving you."

She wanted to lie but couldn't.

Heather pressed her fingers to her mouth, MJ shook her head. Denser smoke poured from Zoe's hair. Becca sagged.

Before things got too bad, Constance figured she better reassure them. "Don't worry. When Gabe asked me out for tonight, I said I had to work till dawn. When he asked about other nights, I told him I never have any free time, making it totally clear we won't be seeing each other again."

"Thank God." Becca pressed her hand to her chest and breathed more easily.

Zoe stopped smoking. Heather's color returned, somewhat. MJ rocked on her heels.

Listless from despair, Constance pushed to her feet and stopped before leaving the room.

Everyone looked at her with compassion, as they would a loser who deserved nothing except pity.

That hurt worse than anything else. "I'm all right." She had no choice except to accept the inevitable. "So are you guys. He won't be back. He surely won't be thinking of me again."

* * * *

Gabe's table at After Dark gave him an excellent view of Constance's building. He understood his need to see her again and his hope she'd come to the landing for some air, no matter how sticky and hot it was. What he couldn't figure out was why he'd wanted to know about this nightspot.

It was no more than a half-ass touristy bar, which meant the music was fair, the drinks watered down, the food bland as Pablum and the crowd too thick for his taste. Twenty-somethings kept bumping into his table as they hurried through the throng, calling out or waving to their equally noisy friends. The older patrons snapped so many pictures with regular cameras, rather than cell phones, countless black spots from the flashes marred his vision.

Nursing his seltzer, he concentrated on the outside area. There were numerous shops, bars, restaurants and people everywhere, as there always was in the French Quarter at night. That deepened the mystery as to why he'd gone to Constance's building and into her office to ask about this place. After Dark was practically across the street, big as fucking life.

More importantly, he was a New Orleans native whose parents still lived in the same parish where he'd grown up. As a cop, he knew this area well, even if new businesses cropped up without warning.

He tried to relax, hoping he could figure it out. Something, possibly a memory, kept nagging him. However, each time the thought floated into his consciousness, it disappeared without giving him an answer. Muttering an oath, he hauled out his notebook and flipped through pages, searching for a clue about tonight. On his last entry, he'd scrawled what could have been a name. Looked like Bicco Sat or Satt.

He should start using his smartphone rather than paper to record this stuff.

He wondered if this Bicco Sat guy owned After Dark and if a snitch had said there was a major drug ring operating from here.

Currently, the only crime was the crappy décor, which included fake leather and pressed wood, along with what they charged for a lousy Cajun burger.

Stumped, he called his snitch and got no answer or voicemail. The turd was probably working another detective in order to pay for his three-thousand-square-foot house. Giving up on him, Gabe called a buddy on the force.

Nathan answered on the second ring. "You still working? Thought you went home."

Gabe tried to recall heading to his condo but couldn't. "Stopped for some food."

"Didn't know you liked Chuck E. Cheese's so much. How can you stand the noise?"

A young woman stood next to Gabe's table and shrieked at some guy near the band. Thankfully, the dude gestured her over.

Gabe turned his back to the crowd. Elderly people crowded the outside walk. The old guys took pictures of babes in short-shorts and bikini tops. Gray-haired ladies snapped his photo through the glass. Gabe lowered his head. "I'm at After Dark."

Laughter burst from the other end. "God, why? There are plenty of other places where you could get a piss-poor meal along with a migraine. Say, McDonald's? At least their fake food is relatively cheap and filling. If you can keep it down."

For someone who'd been known to brown-bag when his funds were low, Nathan could be a real food snob. "You through?"

"Hey, just trying to be a friend here."

"Good. I need you to look up Bicco Sat or Satt for me." He spelled the last name both ways.

"Bicco what?" Nathan chuckled. "Sounds like a male stripper. Didn't know you were into those kinda things. You keep surprising me, man."

He was doing that to himself, too, and didn't have the memories to tell him why. Edgy, he drummed the table. "I'm thinking Satt might own this place." The only thing that could explain his interest in it. "By the way, everyone here is basically clothed. At least enough not to get arrested. See if we have a sheet on him."

"He do something wrong?"

"That's what I'm hoping you can find out."

"Hold on." After a brief lull, Nathan returned. "Nope. He's not in the system."

"Find out if he owns After Dark."

"Give me a sec."

It took longer. Gabe finished his seltzer in the interim.

"Okay, here you go." Phones rang on Nathan's side. "A place called Fun Drinks & Eats owns it. Bicco Satt isn't mentioned anywhere. The company is headquartered in...ah...Delaware. The manager where you happen to be is Chien Pham. No record."

That solved nothing, especially why Gabe had asked Constance about this place. "You're sure?"

"Yeah. Why wouldn't I be?"

"No reason. Thanks. Bye—wait." He wanted to ask why he'd ended up in the French Quarter tonight. Could be Nathan knew. However, whether Gabe should quiz him on that was another matter.

Muted conversation sounded on the other end. Nathan cleared his throat. "Hey, man, you still there? Or did you decide to have a good time at that place?"

He couldn't ask what he wanted. Nathan would wonder why Gabe had forgotten an investigation as if it hadn't existed. Word might get out how he was losing it. Nathan wouldn't blab on purpose, but cops were always ribbing each other about stuff. The more painful the better, like a buddy not getting his cock up for the ladies or the first time a teenage girl called him grandpa.

Unwilling to risk it, Gabe forced a chuckle. "Having a good time here isn't going to happen. See you tomorrow." Before Nathan could answer, Gabe killed the call.

A waitress hurried over. "Hey, I'm Vicki. With an I. I'm taking over for Jacqueline. You ready to order?" Vicki was mid-twenties or so, quite pretty, her hair dark blonde, her smile eager but also predatory, saying she was interested in them getting to know each other better.

Constance's ripe figure, silky hair and sultry scent flooded his thoughts. His cock jumped to attention, telling him he wasn't only hungry for her, he was damn deprived and couldn't leave this area now. He didn't want to. "I'll have the jambalaya and a NOLA Blonde, if you have it."

"We do." She stroked the table near his arm. Her fingers crept closer. "We have lots of stuff."

Rather than inquire about particulars, he handed over the menu Jacqueline had left him.

Vicki's flirtatious mood wilted a bit then rebounded to red-hot. She winked. "Be right back. Don't miss me too much."

At any other time, he might have chatted her up, and if they proved compatible, asked her out for a good time and uncomplicated sex. Not tonight.

He wanted more. He craved Constance. For some reason, the few minutes they'd spent together imprinted her on his brain better than women he'd dated for months or years. Even with those long-lasting relationships, he'd never been close to commitment. Once his girlfriends realized there'd be no engagement ring or wedding in the future, they cut out. He couldn't blame them and he hadn't been sorry. He'd had a good time while it lasted, but he'd been looking for more.

His gut and good sense told him that couldn't be Constance. He didn't know her. Given her work schedule and how she turned him down, he might never see her again. His spirits plunged.

Flashbulbs went off in his face.

Vicki banged on the glass and shouted, "That's not allowed. You're bothering the customers." She joined him. "Honestly, tourists. Here you go." She delivered his beer and food. "This should perk you right up."

"Thanks. I have to get this." Even though his smartphone hadn't buzzed, he brought it to his ear. "Hey, thanks for getting back to me. How's it going?"

When his 'call' didn't end, Vicki drifted to her other tables.

To keep her away, he pretended to listen to someone who wasn't there and ate without tasting a bite, his attention consumed by the door to Constance's office, his anticipation building that she might come out.

An hour later, two horribly pale guys exited, followed by another who needed a shave. Gabe had never seen anyone with so much facial hair. Head down, the hairy guy hurried away. The pale ones licked their incisors.

Weird, but the only thing going down. A half-hour later, Constance still hadn't exited the place.

"Sir?" A middle-aged Asian guy stood next to Gabe's table.

He lowered his water glass. "Yeah?"

"You need to pay your bill and go." He spoke perfect English. "You've been at this table for hours. We have other customers waiting."

This had to be Mr. Pham. Gabe considered showing his badge to get him to back off, but didn't. He had no real business here, except wanting to see Constance and figure out why he'd come to this area in the first place.

"You bet. Sorry for hogging the table." He settled his bill, giving Vicki a thirty-percent tip.

"Please come back." She bounced in place, cheeks flushed. "When you do, ask for me. Don't forget, Vicki with an I."

Outside, Gabe faced the building where Constance worked. A shadow fell across the shuttered window. Whether it was from a male or female, he couldn't tell. The ferns hanging beneath the balcony swayed in the muggy breeze. For some reason, they reminded him of the hairy guy who'd left earlier. Gabe couldn't imagine why and it drove him nuts.

On the way home, he tried to recall whatever he seemed to have forgotten but couldn't. In his kitchen, he picked up the salt shaker, not understanding why the grains fascinated him.

After ditching his clothes, he stretched naked on his bed and stroked his cock as he figured Constance would have done if she'd joined him tonight. She wasn't into being coy or playing games, her kiss more than proved that.

His breath caught.

She'd kissed him first, even apologized, sort of, for having attacked him.

Other memories returned—his tongue in her sweet, hot mouth, Constance sucking it, wanting him as much as he did her.

His balls tightened, needing to release their load. He stroked harder, faster too, wanting to come. He recalled cupping her ass and pushing her cunt into his erection, letting her know he was in command even though she said she ran the place where she worked.

Gabe stilled. A memory neared then zipped away.

He swore. "Come on. Remember, dammit." He tried to will the moment into his consciousness. Something about him being in charge, but Constance also wanting to take the lead...or telling him so.

Gabe bolted to a sitting position, his pulse sprinting. She'd called herself Constance Salt and said she owned the business, but it had been Becca Salt, not Bicco Satt, he'd been looking for. That's why the salt shaker had riveted him, trying to prod him into remembering what he recalled now.

Becca owned the business he'd been investigating on his own after a parish priest had spoken to him about it. Gabe had gone there tonight to check out Father Archambault's strange concerns and to talk to Becca.

Had he?

Gabe tried to recall but the memory remained elusive. Ever since Constance had kissed him, he'd somehow forgotten everything, which made no sense whatsoever. No person could have such an effect on him, not even her. She was a dynamite woman but didn't have the power to fry his brain. His balls maybe, but his gray matter, no fucking way.

He prayed he hadn't had a minor stroke tonight or a fit where he'd participated in stuff but didn't remember anything afterward.

Worried, he left his bed and fired up his laptop. He keyed in what he was beginning to remember, just in case he forgot it again.

Chapter Three

Several days later, the gang surprised Constance with a party to celebrate her fifth anniversary at the service.

It was three months before her original hire date, but she didn't contradict them. They'd gone to a lot of trouble to make her feel wanted and loved.

Heather had hung skulls, conjure dolls, feathers and chicken feet in Constance's office. In other words, voodoo hoodoo decorations or mortal trappings supernaturals knew were downright silly. Zoe lit countless candles, making the room almost as bright as fluorescent lights would. The incense was so thick, Constance struggled to breathe. Didn't matter. MJ conjured up more.

She slipped her arm through Constance's. "How's it going?"

Given that she didn't have a huge hickey on her neck as MJ did, not so good. "I'm great. You?"

"Hey, I'm free. Doesn't get better than that. Actually, I don't know how I lasted so long in the ring. At times, I still have kinks in my back from the confined space."

She stretched, catlike, and blew out a sigh. "Enough about me. There's a lovefest going on this weekend. Heather and Daemon refuse to attend, since messing around with everyone is part of the rules. They want to stay exclusive. Different strokes, you know? Would you like to come? It's gonna be a blast."

Not with MJ snaring all the guys with her effortless sensuality. Even if she hadn't been so much competition, Constance didn't have the heart to mess around. "Thanks, but I think I'll pass. Like I said before, I'm not into orgies."

"Honestly? I thought you said that to keep from upsetting Becca. I love her to death, but she can be a real prude at times."

"If you keep your clothes on and don't jump the clients, she'll be fine."

MJ snickered. "Where's the fun in that?" She waved down Heather. "Hey, I found some new leatherwear. Want to see?"

"Of course."

They huddled together near the desk, whispering and giggling. Pleased with what MJ came up with, Heather shot over to Daemon and showed him what was on the smartphone.

Becca stepped inside holding a humongous molten lava cake on a silver tray.

There wasn't a dessert around that Constance liked better. Everyone's sweet kindness was too much. She wept.

Daemon, Stefin, Anatol and Taro took one look at her damp cheeks and edged back, bumping into each other. In the small space, they looked even taller and bigger than they were. They watched her, their emotions guarded.

Constance waved her hand in front of her face to stave off her emotions. "Don't worry about me. I'm fine. These are happy tears."

Daemon looked at Heather for confirmation. She wept when she was sad, elated, frustrated or just because she was a good fairy and super sensitive.

Always the diplomat, she avoided commenting and instead patted his flat belly.

He was built like a Greek god, and handsome as sin with shoulder-length brown hair and bad-boy stubble. He hung his arm over Heather's shoulder then rested his palm smack on her boob.

She elbowed him hard and shook her head.

He gave her a baffled look but stopped playing with her nipple and dropped his hand to her waist.

Anatol, Stefin and Taro were more circumspect in their carnal hunger for Zoe. They didn't touch her, but the flames in their eyes blazed. Tonight, she'd worn a skintight black dress, a perfect complement to her raven hair and snowy skin. A far cry from the Catholic schoolgirl outfits she'd used to wear before falling in love with the guys.

Lucky girl had three to Constance's zero.

Longing hit her with ruthless force, snatching her breath.

Becca glanced from Constance to the Unholy Trio. All were hotties. Stefin, tall and nicely muscular, his complexion bronze, his blond hair longish. Anatol had mahogany-colored skin and delicious dreadlocks. Taro was as different from the others as they were from him, given his baby blues and auburn hair. They were a testament to the power of testosterone, each guy virile to the extreme.

They backed farther away from Becca, hands clasped innocently behind them, which somehow emphasized the impressive bulges between their legs. Zoe was going to get lucky tonight, possibly in the break room if her guys remained true to form.

Constance ached with envy.

"Happy anniversary." Becca offered a hesitant smile. "We're so glad you're part of our team. Here." She shoved the cake at Constance.

Too bad chocolate wouldn't make everything better tonight.

Daemon hurried to the treat, hungry as always. MJ and Heather grabbed his arms and hauled him back. Again, he gave them a what-did-I-do look.

He was so cute and clueless Constance smiled through her tears. After blowing out the candles, she cut the cake in equal portions, plopped the oozing messes on plates and offered everyone their fair share.

Heather made certain Daemon fed himself and didn't lick her fingers, lips or other body parts.

Zoe stayed across the room from her guys. They gave her smoldering looks.

If Eric had been here, rather than helping a client at his financial firm, Becca might have warned him to behave. Considering he was Cupid's descendant, with impeccable manners and a romantic nature, he wouldn't have had much trouble complying.

Constance welled up. Their sympathy for what she was going through made her feel even lonelier. When they went home tonight, it would be with or to someone. All she had waiting for her was an empty apartment, romance novels, adult films or Internet chat rooms. None satisfied for long.

The others ate and loosened up, their conversation and laughter growing loud.

Becca slipped her arm around Constance's waist. "I have a surprise."

Constance wasn't certain she wanted to hear it. "You're pregnant?"

Becca blushed worse than Heather usually did. "Ah, no. The surprise is for you, not about me."

"Oh. A raise?"

"Uh-uh." She looked embarrassed. "You'll get one, like you always do on your work anniversary, though not tonight." She smiled weakly then brightened. "We have a new client. A demon. Tall, tan and totally in charge, if you get my drift."

Constance wasn't brain-dead. "You're fixing me up?" She sagged. "Please don't tell me you paid the guy to come here."

"No — *no*." Becca waved her hands. "I just thought you'd like to meet him. See if you two hit it off. I swear, he's a client. He booked a spot before you met...ah..."

"Gabe." How easily his name rolled off Constance's tongue when she didn't want it to. She should be grateful for Becca's help and eager to meet a new man, but she felt gun-shy. Blind dates, mixers, fix-ups and hookups had never worked before and surely wouldn't now. At this point, even orgies wouldn't have panned out. "Thanks, but I'd rather not."

"You're sure?" Becca looked past her.

Framed in the doorway was a tall guy with classical Greek features, wavy brown hair, bristly cheeks, a muscular bod to tempt even the most reluctant pussy and flames wiggling in his dark eyes.

Becca pressed close. "That's Farron."

Constance's mouth went dry at his male beauty, her reaction more knee-jerk than anything.

He approached with the assurance of a heat-seeking missile, her as his target.

For the first time ever, she stepped away from a man and not only because of his sulfur scent, the same as

Zoe's, Daemon's, Anatol's, Taro's and every other demon's. Even with all the incense in here the odor still came through.

Crowding her, he took in her ivory turban and matching off-the-shoulder gown. "Hey, how you doin'?"

Not good, considering he sounded like Joey from *Friends*. She didn't trouble over whether Farron used cuffs in bed. Shackles, collars, chains and whips were likely his style. He'd probably show her BDSM moves she never knew existed and give her screaming orgasms but little else.

She was well-acquainted with his kind of man, or rather, demon. They didn't stick around for real intimacy. There were too many other conquests to be had. Already, he eyed MJ, Zoe and Heather. If Constance had to guess, she'd say he liked Heather's innocent appearance the most, believing she'd be a true challenge in his bed.

Poor dude hadn't a clue what a sex fiend Heather could be when her clothes came off. More than once, Daemon had dragged in there looking like death warmed over, but his smile was goofy and wide.

Becca wiggled her eyebrows.

Constance guessed that was her cue to get to know him.

She wasn't into it tonight but had to make an effort since everyone had done so much for her. Braced for the worst, she tapped his shoulder. "Hey."

Sadly, Farron gave her his full attention. He studied her boobs for an indecently long time and even licked his lips as if she were tonight's entrée. Little wonder he'd come here to suppress his beast. He'd have a long way to go before they could set him loose on an unsuspecting world.

He was nothing like Gabe. His interest had simmered beneath the surface and flared briefly. She guessed, or hoped, that was because he couldn't contain his attraction to her. His struggle to remain civilized had made her heart turn over. She'd always been the one pursuing guys. How nice to have them, or rather him, give chase.

Farron came on so strong he made her sweat, and not in a good way.

"Why don't you have some cake?" Becca shooed him away then pressed her mouth to Constance's ear. "After his treatments, he'll be as civilized as the others, I swear."

She figured Becca was referring to the clients, not the guys in here. Daemon had pinned Heather against the wall, arms above her head. He kissed her deeply. Stefin, Taro and Anatol had sandwiched Zoe between them and feasted on her. Taro sucked her neck. Anatol brushed his lips over her ear. Stefin thrust his tongue between her lips.

Even MJ got in on the festivities. She faced the laptop and whoever she'd Skyped. Slowly, she unbuttoned her blouse for the dude.

Everyone moaned, groaned or panted.

Constance went dizzy from panic, not arousal. The first time the promise of hot sex had unglued her. "Thanks." She kept her voice low. "However, I think I'll wait until Farron's through with the program before I give him a whirl."

She grabbed her cake and smiled wanly at him. "Nice meeting you."

"We've just gotten started. Trust me." He dropped his plate, wrapped his arm around her waist and pulled her into him. His erection was gargantuan, his skin super-heated like every demon's was.

She shivered. "What are you doing?"

His hips rocked, which also ground his cock into her. "Dancing."

"There's no music."

He brushed his mouth over her ear. "We'll make our own."

Becca grabbed Constance's plate and mouthed, 'go on, have fun'.

That was like telling a homeschooled kid to play with the Crips, one of the deadliest gangs in America. Constance was no virgin, but this…

Farron danced her around the room, his steps surprisingly decent, his fingers roaming.

She yanked his hand from her ass. "A little advice. Don't go below the waist."

"You got it." He cupped her boob.

If she hadn't known better, she would have thought he'd taken lessons from Daemon. "That's off-limits too."

"Not a prob." He slanted his mouth over hers and plunged his tongue inside.

Her arms flailed.

He deepened his kiss. It was nothing like Gabe's.

She stomped on Farron's toes and pounded on his shoulders.

He groaned. The noise sounded turned on.

Stumped for a solution, she grasped his skull.

"Whoa." Becca gripped his arm and tugged him away. "No need to take his memories."

Constance smoothed her gown. "I beg to differ. I plan to take mine, too."

Several locks hung over his forehead. He grinned lewdly. "That was good. Ready for seconds?"

Before he could tackle her, she fled her office, locked herself in the ladies' john and waited until her party was over before she returned.

Thankfully, she had back-to-back clients during the following hours, making it impossible for Becca and the other ladies to ask her anything personal. Their footfalls sounded in the hall repeatedly and always halted by her closed door. However, none knocked or opened it.

If Farron had truly lusted after her, rather than wanting a warm bod in his bed, he probably would have kicked down the door or used his dark power to vaporize it. She was relieved he hadn't. He was a great-looking dude but didn't own the tenderness she needed. A man with a soul who would care for her just as she was, imperfect and wanting. Despite her imperfections, he'd give his all.

Looked like tonight would be another search for Mr. Perfect in her chat rooms, since no online dating service catered to a voodoo priestess with a needy heart.

The moment her last client left, Constance prayed she could escape the office without anyone stopping, quizzing or feeling sorry for her.

Becca's previous worry about unwanted mortals or cops barging in here hadn't had a lasting effect on Heather. She wasn't at the front desk guarding the castle entrance, so to speak. The closed-circuit monitor proved no one was on the landing, eager to hurry inside. The halls in here were also deserted, everything quiet thanks to MJ's soundproofing.

Constance figured Heather was in the supply closet, going at it with Daemon, or she was in a treatment room, healing a client's bruises, scrapes and broken bones courtesy of the enforcement team.

With her purse wedged beneath her arm, she slipped out of the front door. On the street below, tourists and locals laughed, talked or shouted. Some waved their arms to get another person's attention.

A thirtysomething couple in a horse-drawn carriage finished their kiss. She rested her palm on the guy's cheek. He buried his face in her hair. They went at each other with renewed passion.

Painful longing constricted Constance's throat.

Crazy, she knew. He might be married to someone else, the woman his long-suffering mistress. Maybe they were trying to rekindle lost love before they gave up and divorced. Even so, the picture they'd created made her yearn.

For years, she'd ignored happy couples to protect her aching heart. Her plan had worked until Becca and the others had gotten involved with their men. A scant two years before, they'd all been single, none having any real hope of finding the right guy. Then bam-bam-bam, the others had fallen like dominoes, leaving her alone and unwanted, except for the lousy dates she endured. Men she'd had to flirt with to get them to even notice her.

Chin lowered, she hurried down the stairs to the walk and wove through the crowd, promising herself, as she always did, to find an apartment well away from the French Quarter. A place she could drive to so vacationing couples wouldn't remind her about the happiness she lacked.

She halted at the curb. Another horse-drawn carriage passed. This one had an older couple inside, their smiles luminous and content. She wished them well and hoped they realized how lucky they were.

The crowd pushed into her. Constance entered the street and halted.

Others brushed past, arms and shoulders bumping her as they would an inanimate object, rather than a voodoo priestess who could give them serious hell if she wanted to.

At the moment, she had difficulty breathing, much less plotting revenge.

Gabe stood in front of After Dark, his attention on her, no one else, his gaze filled with unendurable longing.

Too many emotions swirled through her, making her sway. She locked her knees to keep standing, mystified as to what he was doing here. Didn't matter. This was a dream come true. The nightmare would come later when she faced the repercussions of seeing him again.

She stopped close enough for them to touch. Even with scents from Cajun food, beer and humanity bombarding her, his fragrance captivated, as intoxicating as she recalled. Fighting dizziness, she leaned closer.

So did he. "Hi."

"Hi." She touched his cheek, loving his stubble and warmth, needing this moment as she hadn't anything else. The world whizzed by with her and Gabe staring at each other and smiling.

Kindness and honor shone in his eyes, strength that allowed a man to be gentle. He didn't leer at her as Farron had. Gabe's gaze caressed, undoing Constance. She didn't care if he was mortal or a cop. Nothing mattered except right now. She melted into him and sought his mouth as he sought hers. Their lips molded to each other. Tongues touched and danced.

Bewitched, she slipped her arm around his shoulder. Gabe not only accepted her caress, he eased her closer and tightened his embrace, making certain she couldn't get away from him.

As strangers passed, she and Gabe kissed. A tender, searching exploration that made her want more.

He deepened his passion, encouraging Constance to give her all.

She couldn't do anything less, mesmerized by his desire no matter the alarms going off in her head.

His strong hold quieted her misgivings. Pressed close, he branded her with his touch and scent.

"Hey," someone next to her shouted. "Matt. Hey, Matt."

"Yo, didn't know you were here tonight." Matt's bellow was louder than the other guy's.

A horse whinnied, women giggled, strains from a band drifted past. The horn wailed and held its highest note.

She and Gabe kissed through the ruckus, their passion artless at times, noisy, too. Didn't matter. To her, what they were doing was beyond beautiful. Breathless, she eased her mouth free for some much-needed air.

He hauled in a breath, pulled off her turban and sniffed her tresses.

The sexiest move any man had ever made with her. For once, she felt coquettish rather than putting on an act. "What are you doing?"

"Smelling you."

Even Nora Roberts couldn't have penned a better answer. Loopy from lust, Constance stroked Gabe's red tie. It would definitely work to secure a woman's wrists to his bed. He had to have a headboard with slats. Nothing else would fulfill her fantasy. "What are you doing here?"

"Waiting for you."

Warmth and desire almost knocked her down. She captured his mouth and slipped her tongue inside, letting him know she'd have her way.

They didn't let go of each other until they both needed a full breath.

After stuffing her turban in his jacket pocket, he laced his fingers through hers. "Are you living with anyone? A man, I mean."

"What?" Of all the questions she might have expected, and there were lots, she'd never anticipated that one. "No."

"Dating someone special?"

She liked where this was going, even though she shouldn't have. "No. Why?"

Gabe ran his thumb over her rings. "Married?"

"Not even close. I'm not going steady, either. You?"

He grinned. "Nope. I'm as single as you appear to be."

She wasn't certain how to interpret his qualifying statement. Like he didn't quite believe what she'd said.

"Have you eaten yet?"

Other than her anniversary cake, she hadn't and shouldn't. This was wrong. Hell, it was crazy. She had her friends to protect. Constance wanted to look back at the office but figured that would be a huge mistake. Gabe might ask why she was curious about the building. "Ah, yes, I have. Eaten, that is."

His expectant look turned to dismay.

He was killing her and making her feel more desired by the second. No matter what advertisements said, women didn't need diamonds. They required a man's full attention and passion. That was the real gift. The other stuff was mere window dressing. "What I had wasn't actual food, like a meal. Just some cake I grabbed for a snack. That was hours ago."

"You must be starving." He squeezed her hand. "During dinner, I promise not to talk about where you work, unless you want to. Then we will."

Horror gripped her. His memories had returned. The truth rang in his cryptic comment and registered in his lushly lashed eyes. She couldn't imagine how much he'd recalled or if her failure to remove his recollections about her had led him back to what else had happened. Afraid to know the truth, she figured he'd tell her anyway while they ate. If she lived through the meal.

Perspiration ran down her back and between her breasts. In another minute, the humidity, unbearable temperature, her fear and endless arousal would have her gown sticking to her like plastic wrap.

She considered bolting but figured it'd prove fruitless. He'd catch up and would ask questions about the business, Becca and the others. Better to control the situation than have him show up unannounced with a warrant. If he did, she'd have to remove every memory he had of the service, her and possibly the French Quarter.

That would leave him a freaking mess when he had to navigate this area. No way could she do anything so awful to him. She had to find out what he had on them and fix it somehow. "Okay."

"To what?"

"Dinner with you, of course." Foolish or not, she did want to be with him tonight. "Are we going to After Dark?"

"It's not what I thought it'd be. I have another place in mind."

He brushed his lips over hers and led her down the street.

Gabe wasn't surprised Constance was a bit unsteady. His pulse still pounded from the enchanting way she'd greeted him—touching his cheek as though he mattered to her, snuggling close to say she enjoyed their intimacy, seeking his mouth with unashamed need.

No matter what she'd claimed about having to work late and constantly, she was making time for him now.

So much gratitude poured through him, he kissed her knuckles.

Her lids fluttered, her mood dreamy. For a split second. With disappointing speed, her caution returned.

Not the reaction he would have liked. When he'd mentioned where she worked, dread flashed in her eyes. Only a fool would think she wasn't hiding something. Funny thing, though, he didn't want to ask her about the business, figuring what Father Archambault had said couldn't be possible. Constance seemed normal even if she worked for a woman who dressed like a harem girl and employed a too-white receptionist who was shy to the extreme.

Wanting to put her at ease, he smiled. "Please tell me you like real Creole food."

Her features softened. "Is there any other kind?"

Gabe didn't know why or how, but damn, she'd been made for him. Laughing, he swooped down for a fast kiss and led her past the tourist hangouts to Pasquets. Not only the best Creole restaurant in the Quarter, but hidden from the usual crowd. "Have you ever been here?" He hoped not. He wanted this to become their place.

"What's here?"

He pointed. The narrow alley they had to pass through ended at a weathered wrought-iron gate.

She pushed to her toes and craned her neck. "Nope. Never seen this area before, except maybe in slasher films. This is where the heroine usually buys it because she'd dumb enough to walk alone in an unlighted area."

"Then it's lucky you have a cop at your side."

Her soft laughter quivered her throat. "You think?"

"I know." He kissed her deeply. Breathlessly.

She gave him tongue like nobody's business.

His skin tingled.

Finished, they both panted, though his was the hardest. "You like movies like that?"

Her lids were still half-mast, her lips wet from him. "Like what?"

"Where the clueless heroine gets offed in alleys."

"Sometimes, but only if the cameraman uses enough light. I hate those films where everything happens in the dark with only periodic flashes to show what's going on."

"I do, too. If you're going to sell me on gore, show it to me."

She slanted him a look. "I bet you liked *Saw*."

"Not as much as the *Hostel* franchise."

"Oh, my God." She gripped his sleeve. "That was so horrible but awesome. Best movies ever."

"I agree." Smiling, he escorted her to the gate. Beyond it was the outside dining area. White linen tablecloths and red umbrellas quivered in the dank breeze. Floral arrangements boasting a single red candle decorated each place setting.

"Wow. This is nice."

Her approving words and smile meant more to him than they should have, given they'd just met. He didn't question his feelings, content to go with the flow. Any woman who loved the *Hostel* movies couldn't have anything bad about her. "Would you like a table by the gazebo or the fountain?"

"The fountain, please. If it's doable." She glanced around. "Looks crowded."

"It won't be once I pull out my badge."

"Aw, come on." She bumped his arm. "You'd really do that?"

To get her the table she wanted, he'd fucking arrest people to clear this place out. These last days had been horrible for him. He'd hung out at After Dark like a stalker, waiting to catch her leaving work but failing until tonight. It wasn't like him to hunt down any woman. However, he couldn't stay away from her. She'd captured something within him and held it hostage. "Yep."

Thankfully, a couple left before he had to prove his macho. After a short wait, they had their table. Numerous flowers and potted plants surrounded the area. The scents were pleasant but none as heady as hers.

Rather than scan the menu offerings, they regarded each other.

She brushed her leg against his.

Gabe smiled more than he had in years.

Girlish shyness passed over her exquisite features. If there had been better lighting out here, rather than candles and lanterns, he might have seen her color deepen, proving his effect on her. She turned his brain to mush and he'd never enjoyed anything more. "What would you like?"

"What do you suggest?"

He hoped she was thinking the same as him—them naked and wrapped in each other's embrace for a long while. The first time he'd been at her office, he thought he'd read her wrong about her interest in him. He hadn't. Tonight couldn't be any different. Even so, they had to get through dinner first. "How about Oysters

Bienville, blackened salmon and, for dessert, brandied apricot beignets with chocolate sauce?"

"Sounds sinfully good."

She had no idea, though he was determined to show her.

Once the waiter delivered their merlot, Gabe tapped his glass against hers. "To a wonderful meal and evening." He hoped the first of many.

After finishing her sip, Constance touched his hand.

A Taser couldn't have jolted him more in the best possible way. His cock went from semi-flaccid to full-on erect in two seconds flat. His balls wanted out of his boxer briefs and against her. He traced her lacquered nails, liking the deep red shade, and moved to her rings. Some were silver, others gold. Several had sparkling gems, possibly the real kind. "Given your taste in movies, don't you worry about getting mugged while you're wearing all this jewelry?"

"Nope. As you said, not with you around."

He offered a playful look. "I'm not always with you."

Her face betrayed her desire and sudden unease.

That threw him. "You okay?"

She offered a smile lovely enough to liquefy his insides, though her affection didn't seem completely guileless.

"What brought you here tonight, besides me?" She leaned closer. "Is this your territory? Do detectives stake out their own areas?"

She made it sound like he and the other guys peed on the ground, marking their space as dogs do. "I go where I'm needed."

"Did you need to go to After Dark the first night we met?"

"No." His simple answer should have encouraged more questions from her.

She regarded him intently and waited.

He supposed for additional information he couldn't offer. No matter how hard he'd tried, and, fuck, he had, he still couldn't recall having asked her about the nightspot as she'd claimed.

A new emotion crossed her face that he couldn't quite read. Since she didn't speak, he had to. "Everything all right?"

"Sure." She squeezed her wineglass. "Are you feeling okay?"

He had been until she'd asked. He recalled his mounting panic the last time they'd been together. Him forgetting stuff he shouldn't have. "Yeah, I'm fine. Why?" He prayed she knew even as he worried what she might say.

She waved her hand. "Just wondering. So, tell me about you. What have you been doing these last days?"

There wasn't a lot he could say, given the cases he was working on, so he lifted his shoulders. "Stuff. You?"

"The same."

Her work was also confidential, which meant they were at an impasse. Rather than drag this out and worry her worse than she already appeared to be, he caressed her fingers. "You want to know why I was at your office the other day and asked to see Becca Salt, don't you?"

Chapter Four

The breeze quieted. Conversations drifted away. Candlelight gleamed in Gabe's eyes, making their color even lighter and unearthly.

He looked beautiful and dangerous, like a fallen angel.

Dizzy, Constance pressed into the chair to steady herself. No way could she claim to be Becca again, unless she was willing to remove his memories once more. If she did and left his recollection of her intact, this same scene would repeat itself endlessly, similar to the dumb film *Groundhog Day*. Gabe would keep remembering stuff he shouldn't and ask her out to see what was up. She'd go. They'd have a great time, except for moments like these. Their dates would lead nowhere, making her beyond bereft straight into suicidal.

She had to leave but couldn't move.

Gabe squeezed her fingers, either in comfort or encouragement.

He was too good, not deserving this. Now Farron and Radagar? Fucking up their memories and watching the fallout was what she'd been born for. She forced herself to speak. "Becca's the greatest."

"I'm sure she is."

She had expected an argument or accusation, not his placid agreement. Maybe he was playing her. It was always possible she'd read him wrong and he wasn't as nice as she'd thought.

Then again…

Tenderness and honesty practically oozed from him, urging her to fess up and beg him to understand.

Constance couldn't fall into that trap. She didn't want to plead with any guy to accept her or her friends as they were when there wasn't anything wrong with them. Having superhuman powers and living forever as demons, fairies and witches did, simply made them unique.

Something a mortal would never appreciate, not even one as nice as Gabe appeared to be. She braced herself for the fight of her life. "I mean it, Becca's a good person."

He smiled. "Exactly what the receptionist said about you."

Good God, he had remembered those moments. No mistaking that now. A sour taste rose to her mouth. She swallowed it down. "Her name's Heather. You'll never meet anyone sweeter."

"Seemed overly shy to me."

"You scared her."

"What? How?" He took himself in. "Am I so awful?"

He looked good enough to eat, his stubble lickable, lips and mouth drool-worthy. She wasn't about to consider his intimate parts. Without clothes, he'd be a freaking god, his cock meaty, balls pendulous. She reined in her desire. "You know you're not."

"Thanks." He kissed her fingertips. "Why did you lie about being Becca?"

Her stomach clenched. "I wanted you for myself." The words tumbled from her mouth before she could stop them. No way would she take them back since they were the damn truth.

Surprise registered on his face, followed by delight and what looked like doubt. "Would she have made a play for me? Does she usually do that with men she doesn't know?"

Constance figured anything she said would dig her deeper. Too bad she couldn't stay silent. "Not as a rule. You're special."

His skepticism returned. He released her hand.

That was a crying shame, since she hadn't lied.

He regarded his wineglass rather than her. "Why didn't you simply offer to answer my questions yourself when we met? By the way, what is it you do at the service?"

"I'm Becca's assistant."

He gave her a sidelong glance. "For real?"

For this conversation. She pretended he'd insulted her. "You don't think I'm capable?"

"Baby, I think you could do whatever you wanted." He stroked her thumb. "And far, far more."

Her belly fluttered. His endearment, touch and the lust flaring in his eyes conquered her too easily. "Thanks. I'm about to celebrate my fifth anniversary there."

"Seriously? Congratulations." He kissed her palm.

It took all the control she owned not to moan in pure pleasure. His silky lips warmed her and his stubble rasped her skin. A spectacular contradiction. When this meal was over and they parted forever, she was going to die.

He glanced up. "So you really wanted me?"

If she confessed how much and that her remaining life would be shit without him, he'd get a swelled head. "Uh-huh."

"Why did Becca go along with your lie and pretend to be Lorraine?"

Constance had forgotten their dumb performance. Fear battered her, making her ill. "Ah, we get a lot of salespeople dropping by unannounced, trying to push office supplies, computer equipment, you name it. Talk about obnoxious. If we let them, they'd never give Becca a moment's peace. I run interference for her. She goes along with it. It's no crime."

"Nope. It's not. But you knew I wasn't a salesman."

He wasn't going to let her win this interrogation. She wanted to disappear but had to at least try to fight. "Your badge could have been a fake. You could have been, too. We've had people say they're all kinds of things to get her attention."

"She's important, huh?"

"She's a great person."

"I'm sure you'd know." He held her hand in his, arousing and imprisoning her.

Constance didn't want to consider the latter but couldn't avoid her worry. She had to know the damage he could cause the place and find some way to avoid or minimize it without hurting him in the process. "Why did you want to talk to Becca? We pay our bills. We're not in trouble with the IRS, city, state, FBI, CIA or any other alphabet group." She made a face and eased her hand from his. "So why are you harassing us?"

"Harassing?" He gestured to their surroundings. "Wait till I tell the guys how I browbeat you here. They'll be so impressed, the next time they need to grill their perps, they'll be sure to make reservations first."

She giggled.

Gabe folded his arms on the table. "Are we friends again?"

If he kept making her smile and turning her on, no telling what they might end up being. Constance wanted to consider the best — them actually dating, falling for each other, having so much trust they could share their deepest secrets, including how she'd removed his memories and would continue to do so if he threatened Becca or the others.

Her and Gabe's love story was never going to happen.

She pushed aside melancholy and touched his arm. "I didn't mean to be critical. Forgive me?"

"Sure." He grinned. "Now ask for something hard."

She wasn't crazy enough to suggest he drop his investigation. "You never answered me about why you came to the service. Why did you? What's this about?"

"I didn't tell you the other day when you brought me into your office?"

He'd recalled that, too. She wanted to be sick. "It was Becca's. I needed to keep up my act just in case you weren't who you said you were. And, no, you didn't tell me then." Her cheeks burned. "We simply kissed."

"I don't remember it being simple at all." He traced her fingers.

Pleasure raced up her arm and dipped to her pussy.

"To be honest, I'm reluctant to say what brought me there."

Her delight evaporated faster than water on a hot skillet. This was worse than she'd feared. He knew every-fucking-thing. How he managed to do so escaped her. More importantly, she couldn't figure out why she'd be here with him if he already had the awful truth. "You expect me to confess?"

"Huh? No." He looked like a cop now, hard and suspicious. "What would you have to confess to?"

"I don't know. You're being so mysterious I'm not sure what I or the others at work did wrong." She threw up her hands. "Are you going to make me guess?"

"Of course not. Calm down, please." He glanced at the other tables.

No one had noticed her outburst. Everyone stuffed their faces and drank up a storm.

Gabe scooted his chair closer to hers. "Do you or any of your colleagues know Father Archambault?"

Sounded like a priest. For Constance, Becca and the rest to be tight with a holy man would be like an evangelical having devil worshippers as BFFs. "I've never heard the name. Why?"

"He's a friend of my parents. Came to see me a few weeks back and asked if I'd look into your service for him. Not as an official investigation, but on my own time."

This was getting weirder by the second. "He asked you to check us out because he wants a makeover so he can date a—ah... So he can score with the babes? I thought the church had a celibacy rule. Has it changed? Is he from another religious group that believes in messing around?"

Gabe's shoulders shook from his laughter. "No. He wasn't asking for himself. He's Catholic, by the way. He said he'd heard things."

Her blood turned to ice. She suppressed a shiver. "What exactly?"

He drained his glass. "More wine?"

She'd barely touched hers and didn't want to know what the good father had heard but had no choice if she wanted to protect the service. "What did he say?"

Gabe bounced his legs like guys do when they don't want to talk.

His information must be epic bad. "Please, tell me. I have a right to know. So do the others who work there."

"It's still hard to say."

The bald truth always was. "I'd rather you not make me wait or guess."

"I'm not trying to do either." He groaned. "Father thinks you're performing animal sacrifices there for some kind of black magic thing."

Constance barked a laugh.

Several patrons stared.

She couldn't have cared less. This was about mortal activities no supernatural would deign to consider. How ludicrous. "I can assure you, we don't do anything with animals there. We're not zoned for it." She giggled.

Gabe didn't share her levity. "He said he heard the animals hissing and howling."

Goose bumps broke out on her arms, despite the oppressive heat. Father Archambault couldn't have known the sounds vamps and weres made unless he'd heard them firsthand, which wasn't possible. There had to be a reasonable explanation for this. She forced herself to play it cool. "Is he mental?"

"More like the most rational person I've ever met. He's all for women's rights, even for ordaining them as priests. Believes anyone who harms a child should do time, no excuses. He's not into magical thinking and doesn't have much patience for those who are, such as cult members who hurt animals in order to raise Satan from the depths of Hell."

Like that would get Satan off his sorry butt when the old fart had other things to do, namely stuff to please himself. "So Father Archambault is lucid. Is he also telepathic? Groans and moans zipped from our place to his head?"

"He said hisses and howls, and, no, they didn't transmit like radio signals. He was in your office."

The world dipped and swayed so much, Constance grabbed her chair to keep from reeling. She couldn't comprehend when he'd been inside or why no one had noticed. "He made an appointment with us and thought he heard these things?"

"He had an appointment at an office in the next building, a nonprofit group for the homeless. He went into your place by mistake. Heard some strange shit — ah, stuff, then took off and came to me."

They should have been locking the front door no matter what Becca said. This had been a fuckup waiting to happen. Collecting herself, Constance struggled for a way to deal with the unthinkable.

Gabe regarded her. "What?"

He would ask that. Now she'd have to tell him something when she wasn't anywhere close to pulling together a logical explanation. "Huh?"

"What? Wait." He held up his hand. "You got an odd look on your face after I told you what Father said. Why?"

"Wouldn't you? Don't you listen to yourself?"

His eyebrows shot up. "Are you mad at me?"

She was scared and liked him too much already, but the outrage angle was her only hope. "Yeah. Do I honestly strike you as the type of woman who would harm any animal? We're not talking spiders or roaches, they're insects. Do you truly believe I'd hurt a bird or mammal in an absolutely ridiculous ceremony to call up a being that doesn't even exist?"

"No. Would Becca?"

Constance tensed. "Absolutely not. She's a wonderful person. Everyone who works there is."

"Then where is the hissing and howling coming from?"

She'd forgotten about the sounds. "Those noises must have come in from the outside."

"How? I heard them in the hall when you and I walked down it."

Bile rose to her throat.

Gabe didn't look much better. Surprise flickered on his face, possibly at what he'd said. He grew thoughtful then confused. "I remember it now." He stared at her. "You and I were walking down the hall and I heard those sounds."

She tried to look concerned rather than stone-cold terrified. "Seriously? Are you sure you're all right?"

"You mean sane rather than nuts?"

"I meant are you working too hard?" She stroked his head pretending to console him, but actually removed the sounds he'd remembered and his memories when they'd walked down the hall.

His face went slack.

She considered zapping his recollections regarding Father Archambault but figured that might backfire later when they spoke. "Everything okay?"

He blinked and squinted at her. "I'm sorry, what were we talking about?"

Nothing she wanted to revisit. "Father Archambault hearing weird noises when he accidentally came into the service."

Gabe nodded slowly. "He seemed insistent. He's not one to overreact to anything. Hell, he served in Iraq and even it didn't unglue him."

"Maybe he was having a bad moment. Happens to everyone." Constance was having hers right now.

"He's not going to be satisfied until I tell him I had a look around."

She started to sweat again. "You mean tonight?" Claw marks decorated the walls in the treatment rooms. Weres, vamps, reapers, demons and no end of other supernaturals roamed freely or were strapped to treatment tables where they howled, shrieked or hissed away. Zoe and her enforcers were demons except for Daemon who was a former satyr. Once Gabe saw or spoke to them, especially Zoe, he'd freak out.

"Why not tonight?" He searched her face. "I wouldn't disturb anyone. I simply want to put Father's concerns to rest."

"No." She spoke without thinking and couldn't back down. "Our clients have a right to their privacy. They're hurting because of how they look and act. They don't need a cop lurking around staring at them."

Particularly if they morphed from their human forms into whatever else they were.

"I wouldn't be intrusive and make them feel bad." He pressed her knuckles to his cheek. "Trust me. I've noticed some of the guys who've left your place. They really do need help, especially the pale and hairy ones."

He'd seen the vamps and weres. Thankfully, they hadn't transformed in front of him as the were had during his initial visit. "Now you know why they need us. Not every man's as lucky as you."

He shook his head. "What do you mean?"

"Oh, come on, you never look in a mirror? You don't see how women drool over you?"

"I'm waiting for you to do it."

She arched one eyebrow.

"Maybe later, huh?" He winked. "I don't want to keep pressing this, but if I don't satisfy Father, he will go to someone else. He's not one to give up."

Gabe wasn't, either. However, if he made Father Archambault wait for an answer and the priest went to someone else that could prove far worse. No way could she remove memories from everyone on every police force without missing a few. "You can't simply tell him you checked us out when you didn't?"

"I'm not that kind of man."

She admired his integrity but worried, too. "The only time you could come by would be before clients arrive. None of us will breach their privacy. I'm not sure Becca will even allow this."

"Will you ask her?"

Constance would rather go on a year-long date with Farron, but she nodded.

Before things got too tense between him and Constance, the twentysomething server arrived with their oysters. Gabe concentrated on the young man, rather than her, hoping she hadn't guessed how he'd lied. Not a lot. Just enough to get inside the office.

He didn't believe anything weird was going on. Father must have been stressed out or misinterpreted normal sounds as hisses and howls. In the halls…

A memory niggled, one Gabe couldn't quite snag. No different from the other day when this happened. The recollection had something to do with the noises Father claimed to have heard. Frowning, Gabe racked his brain and tried to snatch details.

"Sir, is everything all right?"

He hadn't realized he'd been staring at the kid. "Yeah, smells great."

Onion, cayenne and other spicy scents wafted toward him. Plump oysters bubbled in their shells, each blanketed by a rich shrimp-and-mushroom sauce browned to perfection.

The young man eased one serving onto a plate for Constance. She didn't bother to look at the appetizer. She observed Gabe, and not in a good way.

Her concern worried him, though not because she thought he was losing his mind. If she was hiding something, like Becca and the others engaging in an illegal activity, Constance was most likely trying to protect them.

He hoped his suspicions were dead wrong.

Troubled, he planned to chat with everyone once he was at the service…the reason he'd lied about Father's tenacity. It was the only way Gabe knew to get in there. He'd be informal, even friendly, so he didn't frighten them, in particular Heather. He certainly didn't need her freaking out on his account. That would kill his and Constance's budding relationship as fast as him telling her he'd been married several times and had twelve kids, each by a different mother. If her friends were up to something, he'd have a long, hard talk with

Constance in order to shield her. As to the others…
He'd do what he could to keep them from too much
shit.

The server left.

Gabe tried to lighten the mood. "Look good?"

She regarded him blankly.

He cut his oyster, slipped his fingers beneath her chin
and brought the food to her lips. "Go on…enjoy." This
was supposed to be their night and their beginning, not
the road leading to the end.

She tongued the morsel into her mouth, chewed and
pressed her hand to her chest. "Oh, my God, that is so
good. Why did you keep this place a secret until now?"

The first time he'd asked her out, she'd turned him
down. Why? His doubt crept back. He shoved it away.
She had to be clean and so did the others. He simply
wouldn't allow any other outcome, nor would he
trouble over it any longer. "I'm an inconsiderate SOB.
Forgive me?"

"Will I get more of the appetizer if I do?"

"Even if you don't, you'll get as much as you want."
He stroked her throat and licked sauce from her bottom
lip.

She wore a dazed look. "I like the way you eat. Show
me how to feed you."

"Are you a fast study?"

"If I'm not, I'll take remedial classes. Promise."

"Deal." As long as those lessons were with him, he
wouldn't complain. He cut another piece, handed her
the fork and parted his lips.

She slipped her hand beneath his chin.

His peripheral vision faded. Never had his heart beat
as fast. A little more of this and he might wind up on
the ground conked out from too much pleasure.

She made a throaty sound, pure female. "Open up."

He already had. His soul wanted to embrace hers. He tongued the morsel off the fork.

Constance scooped up sauce, licked the tines and shivered. "Damn, that is outstanding. I'm going to ask the chef for his recipe."

"Yeah?" Gabe couldn't help but chuckle. "Lots of luck in getting it." He fingered sauce from his mouth.

"Here, let me." She licked his digit clean.

The only way this moment could have been better was if she'd tongued his cock. "You know how to cook?"

"Sure. Open up a can and use the microwave. Even a child could manage that."

"I believe that's because it's called heating stuff."

"You know, I never realized pressure cookers could explode." She ate another oyster then gave him one. "A few years back, I got hooked on one of those cooking channels and decided I had to make custard. Trust me, it's easier to buy it already finished. I'm still not sure what I did wrong, but some of that stuff is still stuck to my ceiling. I would have had to buy a ladder to scrape it off and didn't want to waste my money on something I'd never use again. Thankfully, the stains almost match the paint."

"No harm done then." He gave her the last oyster. "When I first started on the force, I had this constant craving for jambalaya."

"If you were a woman, I would have suspected you were pregnant."

"Yeah. Glad I wasn't. Anyway, I started to experiment with recipes to get them just the way I liked. Lots of heat."

"I'm sensing this story has an unhappy ending. How'd things turn out?"

"To this day, my eyes water when I think of the seasoning I used. I'm just glad I didn't permanently destroy my taste buds."

She wagged her fork. "That'll teach you to mess with recipes. Those things are written in stone."

"Hey, if you can't live dangerously… Besides, I have a cast iron stomach, or did until then."

"How do you feel about chocolate?"

He toyed with lying to please her but wouldn't. Conversing with Constance felt good. Free and comforting, the way a man and a woman should behave. No BS or dumb games. Simply two people getting to know each other and liking what they learned. "Even as a kid, I couldn't eat it. Nothing beats vanilla."

"I can't believe you just said that. You must be running a fever." She pressed her palm against his forehead. "Just as I thought. You're burning up and hallucinating."

He cuffed her wrist and pressed her hand to his chest. "I swear I won't hold it against you about liking chocolate. I think that's a component in female DNA. Nothing you can do about it."

She licked sauce from her lips. "Is that a sexist comment?"

"Nope. Merely an observation. Remember, I'm a detective. I have the badge to prove it."

"About that. Is your number 007?"

He fell back laughing. "Not hardly. How do you feel about sports?"

"Is this a trick question?" She narrowed her eyes. "Are you waiting for me to groan?"

"Hope not."

Her grin lit up her face. "I'll watch any basketball game even if preschoolers are playing but football totally sucks."

Gabe figured he'd have to sway her to his side so they could watch the Super Bowl together. "Besides horror flicks, you ever watch stuff on TV?"

"Only basic things."

"The news, weather…"

"More like *Suits, Grey's Anatomy* and *Nashville.* I bought every season so I could re-watch them when I wanted." She pointed. "I am not addicted."

He held up his hands in appeasement. "I'll never say you are. I like *Suits,* even though I can't believe any major New York firm would hire a guy who didn't have a law degree, not even one from an online university. Talk about unrealistic. How about *The Walking Dead*? You into that?"

She sipped her wine. "When they take it off the air, I'm going to have a meltdown. I might even write my Congressperson."

A woman after his own heart. "For me, it's the best show ever."

"Agreed, even if zombies in real life are nothing like what they portray."

He lowered his glass. "What?"

She blinked then flushed. "Huh?"

They were back to that? "What do you know about zombies?" He laughed awkwardly. "Especially in real life."

"Are you serious?" She gave him a look that said he'd lost his mind. "I meant in plays and things. The way the show depicts them is one way but they have computer software to show them crawling around when their legs are gone and their guts are hanging out. You can't do that on stage or as a Halloween costume."

"True. About books…"

By the time their entrées arrived, he'd admitted some romances weren't bad, they both agreed Lawrence Sanders wrote dynamite thrillers and neither of them liked sci-fi except for *Brave New World*. Police procedurals got two thumbs up.

"I dare you to name anyone who writes true crime better than Wambaugh." His hero.

"I can't because that person doesn't exist." She kissed his palm, and he hoped she was unconcerned if the server or the other diners noticed. That only he and she mattered.

They shared from each other's plates to see who'd gotten the choicest piece. He hadn't a clue, not tasting what she slipped into his mouth. He was too enthralled with her, wanting to know everything and then some. So far they'd only skimmed the surface with inconsequential stuff. "Are you a native of this area?"

"Family has been here for generations."

So had his. "Your mom and dad live in this parish?"

Constance tasted the salmon and released a pleasured sigh.

The sounds she made so effortlessly…wow. Desire tightened his throat, keeping him from swallowing.

She speared more fish.

Surprised, he repeated his question about her parents, guessing she hadn't heard him during her culinary orgasm.

Her chews slowed. She perused the food.

Doubt ate at him. He pushed it away and told himself she was simply enjoying their meal, not evading his conversation. Determined to give her a chance, he waited.

She touched her napkin to her lips. "My parents live in Saint Tammany. But they're rarely around. Their house I mean. Both of them retired early and they travel a lot."

"What did they do?"

She stilled, but hid her disquiet and smiled. "Teachers—for private schools all over the area. They went where they were needed."

The exact words he'd used when telling her about his job. What a coincidence her folks had the same setup. That is, if they were teachers. The cop in him was back and growing increasingly suspicious. Gabe warned himself to knock it off. He had no right to know about her private life. Could be her parents were trolls and she didn't want to admit it. However, he was still eager for some information. "I know what I'm about to ask sounds silly, given how we're sharing this meal and those wonderful times we've kissed. But I don't know your last name. What is it?"

She downed half her wine before coming up for air. "Seriously, I didn't tell you? We have been bad." She gave him the once-over, lingering on his mouth, chest and what she could see of his lap covered by his napkin. "It's Chastain."

"Beautiful. The same as you."

Longing transformed her features followed by deep despair.

Alarmed, he touched her wrist. "What's wrong?"

"Nothing."

Her eyes sparkled more than they should. He suspected she was going to cry.

Constance dismissed her sorrow, or whatever it had been, and resumed eating like nothing had happened.

This had to be about her parents or family. Maybe they were worse than trolls, even criminals with sheets longer than his snitches. His being a cop might have made her reluctant to share bad stuff about her people. He couldn't ask outright but was willing to dance around the subject and coax her to open up.

Strolling musicians stopped at the table and played a romantic piece on their violins, killing any chance for him or her to share histories.

She pressed her knee against his.

He forgot his questions and stroked her fingers. Her hair was so dark it had a slight blue sheen. The candlelight made her seem like a vision rather than a real woman. Her pale gown resembled what ladies wore in this area centuries ago.

Although he knew too little about her, it was as if they'd dated forever, his reaction as much emotional as physical. He still harbored concerns about the service and her folks, but he was also oddly at peace. A feeling that had never happened with a woman he'd just met or those he'd known for years.

The musicians ended their tune.

Gabe gave them a generous tip.

The beignets arrived buried beneath powdered sugar. A taste delight.

Constance didn't touch hers.

That wouldn't do. He wanted to give her everything. "Would you like something else?"

She nodded.

He thought back to the menu. "Bananas Foster?"

She shook her head.

"Bread pudding? Pralines? Both?"

"No, no and no."

Gabe chuckled. "I've run out of choices. What do you want?"

"You. Take me to your place tonight. Please."

Chapter Five

It was reckless for Constance to ask Gabe for an intimate night, but she didn't care. This was her one chance to be with him. A man she'd never expected to meet or would get to know and enjoy for more than one evening.

The reality was so crushing she couldn't deny herself any longer. As soon as their time was over, she'd have to plant false memories of him touring the service and finding it blander than an Osmond TV special. Once he'd set Father Archambault's mind at ease, she'd erase Gabe's recollection concerning the place and her, leaving him to his future and another woman. While they celebrated their newfound love, Constance would yearn.

Unaware of her turmoil, he brightened. "I thought you'd never ask. Just give me a sec." He gestured for the server. "Want to take the beignets with us?"

"Not if you have a rule against eating in bed."

"Are you kidding? As far as I'm concerned, we shouldn't eat anywhere else." He kissed her hard and deep, his passion so real she never wanted to leave his embrace.

Gabe caught his breath and handed the beignets to the server. "We'll take these with us. I'm ready for the bill. We're in a hurry."

He had no idea. She could barely keep from jumping out of her skin. Need ate at her, taking too many pieces from her heart. She kissed his fingertips. "I'm glad we ran into each other tonight."

"Me, too. Can I ask you something?"

She wished he wouldn't. "Sure."

"Given the good time we've had so far and the one we've yet to have, why'd you turn me down the first time?"

She'd forgotten about that. Funny how his memories were more enduring than hers even though she'd zapped him several times. "You caught me off guard. You were a stranger."

He got a funny look on his face. "That didn't stop you from kissing me."

Her face burned. She hoped he didn't notice. "We were where I worked. What could you do?"

"You mean to you? Like hurt you?"

That was one worry she'd never have around him, at least physically. When she fell off the precipice into complete despair it would be because she'd run from him, not the other way around. "I guess I was gun-shy. I'd just come off a bad relationship. It ended a couple of months ago."

Understanding filled his eyes. "He didn't…"

"No. Nothing physical. He cheated."

"I'm sorry." He cradled her face. "You deserve better."

They both did. The truth for one. How she wished she could be straight with him.

"Here you go, sir." The server returned with the boxed beignets and the bill.

Gabe signed the receipt quickly. They raced from the dining area to his car in a no-parking zone.

"Bad boy." Snuggled close, she rubbed her boobs against his chest. "Better watch it or you'll get towed."

"No one would dare." His voice had dropped an octave. "I'm a cop."

Constance couldn't imagine anything more exciting. She ran her fingers down his tie to his belt, but stopped before reaching the precious cargo behind his fly. "Did you bring your cuffs?"

Untamed desire intensified his features. He swooped down and kissed her so greedily she had to restrain herself from pushing him to the asphalt and crawling all over him.

They made out in his car, not bothering to come up for air.

Something banged on the window.

She flinched.

Male laughter rang out. "Hey, you two should get a room."

Several wolf whistles pierced the other noise.

If only she had Zoe's power to nuke obnoxious guys. She gripped Gabe's lapels. "Arrest them."

"It'd take too long." He kissed her throat.

She slipped further beneath his spell. "Then shoot them, please."

"I'd rather do that to you."

"With your special equipment?"

"You bet. Hold on." He drove like a maniac to his place, weaving around slower vehicles and zooming through yellow lights.

Constance stroked his balls and cock.

"Holy fuck." He gritted his teeth and gripped the steering wheel. "That's pissing awesome."

Her thoughts exactly. She would have unzipped his pants and released his shaft but worried he might hit something. The crappy paperwork he'd have to fill out would delay their joy.

He parked smack between two spaces at an upscale condo development, rushed her to the front door and pressed her against the wood. While he ground his groin into her pussy, he fumbled with the lock.

Coming home like this each night would be glorious. If MJ could have delivered that wish, Constance would have paid everything she had to get it.

Once inside, he kicked the door closed and turned the deadbolt.

Refreshingly cool air enveloped her.

He flicked on the lights. Handcuffs dangled from his thumb.

A voodoo priestess couldn't have asked for better. Nor could a woman. She dropped her purse.

His kiss was more savage than the others. She pulled at his clothes. He tore at hers. The pastry bag crinkled and the cuffs tapped her in various places. He didn't drop, either.

They stumbled down the hall, their kisses noisy and enduring.

Gabe pulled her into a room, broke free and hit the lights.

His bedroom was neat yet masculine. Photographs depicting faraway places graced the walls. A dark, chunky dresser and leather chair stood to one side, the area mostly dominated by his big bed, just long enough for him. It had an awesome mahogany headboard.

She held back a squeal. "You have slats."

He looked over. "By God, I do. I'd never noticed." He dropped the bag on the nightstand and pulled a string of condoms from the top drawer. "I have other things, too." He swung the rubbers like a pendulum. "You are now in my power. Do not look away. Do not—"

Her laughter drowned him out. Constance couldn't recall a time she'd behaved so silly, nor had so much fun. "How many are there? Will there be enough?"

"Let me check." Gabe counted those he held and the ones in the box. "Think we'll use forty tonight?"

He must have just cracked open the package. "I'm willing to try if you are." She kicked off her high-heel slides.

He grinned at their leopard-skin print then sobered. "Not so fast."

Her hands stalled on her gown. Worn off the shoulder, it wouldn't take a lot to push the thing off. "You want to go slow? Seriously?" Unable to breathe or think, she was well past the point of no return.

He was as close as a man could get to drooling. "I want you to strip then undress me."

"You're beyond bad."

The cuffs dangled from his thumb. "Let's see."

She liked the way he played. To toy with him, she ran her fingertips over her neckline. "Sure you still want to go slow?"

Rough breathing wiggled his tie. His cock thickened and pushed against his pants. "If you rush, there will be hell to pay."

He had to be talking about a spanking. This was too damn wonderful. Once it had ended, she was going to be a hopeless mess. She should have raced out of the door. Instead, she surrendered to real pleasure, as she'd never done with another man. With Gabe, she didn't have to act like a sex fiend in order to pump up her passion or keep his interest. She wanted him, and by God, he felt the same about her.

Because he hadn't a clue what she really was and did for a living.

Her worry returned. Rather than dwell on it, she eased out of her gown. The lightweight silk slid past her boobs, waist, hips and thighs to puddle at her feet.

He gaped at her black bodysuit. The color matched her skin. Sweetheart cups displayed her breasts seductively.

She kicked her gown aside, pivoted and struck a cheesecake pose like those shown during the nineteen-fifties. The thong back revealed her naked ass.

A noise poured from him that she'd never heard from another man, arousal at its finest. He stared at her butt cheeks, his arms hanging limply at his sides, the cuffs dropped and forgotten.

Bursting with confidence, she lowered the side zipper inch by inch and faced him. The bodysuit fell away from her breasts. Her nipples were so erect from his attention and the coolish air they stung pleasantly, aching for his mouth and tongue.

He prowled toward her and stopped.

She wasn't certain why. Maybe he didn't want to rush or his legs wouldn't work any longer. Didn't matter. If it killed them both, they were going to have this night.

She ditched her bodysuit. Naked and unashamed, she let him look his fill.

His color heightened. He loitered on her curly bush and delicate folds, already damp from her desire for him.

Bliss awaited them. "Now it's your turn."

Gabe reached for her.

She caught his wrists but couldn't circle them. They were too thick. "Don't move."

"Are you kidding?"

"Wait till I've undressed you then do whatever you want. And I do mean whatever."

Veins popped out on his forehead. If he got any more excited, he'd explode. He tried to tongue her nipple.

"Uh-uh." Constance leaned away. "You're still dressed."

He muttered an oath. "Fine. I'll help you."

"Nope. That's not what you said."

"Screw what I said."

She tightened her grip. "Let me do it my way. Please." She had to make this last and savor these moments for the lonely days ahead. If she'd been wise, she would have recorded this on her smartphone, a memento she'd have for a lifetime. Sometimes memories weren't enough.

He blew out a breath. "Don't go too slow unless you want to kill me."

She'd be right behind him, missing out on this pleasure. "Wouldn't think of it."

She brushed her lips over his temple then eased his jacket off his shoulders and arms. The garment fell and rustled at his feet. Her pounding pulse nearly masked the sound. His shoulder holster and gun seemed enormous and deadly, yet wildly masculine, too. Unable to resist, she stroked the grip and leather. "We'll come back for this later. Right now, I want to see your real weapon."

He laughed.

The best sound the world offered. Constance didn't know how she'd live without such joy or his rich, deep voice that thrilled yet comforted.

She shouldn't have let things get this far. Nothing could make her stop.

On her knees, she undid his belt. The metal clink from the buckle and the rasp from his zipper generated outrageous X-rated fantasies that rivaled every erotic romance she'd read. Nothing beat the real deal. Heat dashed through her, the warmth settling in her pussy. A pulse ticked deep within, an invitation for his cock.

She resisted her unruly arousal to take this as slow as she could. Undressing him was like opening a longed-for gift she'd never believed existed.

It didn't really. A man like him wasn't made for a voodoo priestess with too many secrets and precious friends she had to protect. Tonight was no more than make-believe on her part...a Cinderella fantasy. Come morning, the wicked witch known as reality would intrude, bringing with it enormous crap she didn't want to consider now.

She lifted her face.

Gabe watched her. His grin proved how much he was enjoying this.

He couldn't imagine the wonders she had in store. She eased her thumbs beneath the waistbands on his pants and navy boxer briefs. God love him, he wore the stretchy kind that were uber sexy. She yanked those suckers down.

His cock sprang out and bobbed between his shirt tails, the shaft rigid as hell, fucking long and thick too.

A perfect specimen of male power, the same as his lightly furred balls. Denied too long, she burned his masculine beauty into her memory. Veins snaked up his rod's impressive length, its color similar to cocoa. His crown proved slightly darker and was decidedly beefy. A delicious mouthful. Pre-cum pearled on the small slit at the top.

She pressed her face into his thick curls and couldn't make one sound given her breathless state. No manufactured scent could surpass his natural musk. If only she could bottle the fragrance and take it with her once this was over.

Despair pressed close. She shoved it away and brushed her lips over his cock.

The precious thing rose to meet her.

There wasn't a chance she'd grumble about that. She explored his narrow hips, hard ass and the furrow between his cheeks.

A strangled sound erupted from him. He pushed to his toes.

She stroked the silky cleft between his butt cheeks and tarried on his tight ring.

"Argh. Shit. That's…" He squirmed.

Surprised by his response, she stopped. "You don't like this?"

"Hell, yeah. It's too fucking great."

That didn't make sense. "So you want me to keep going? Or would you like me to —"

"Do it, do it, *do it*…please."

"Absolutely." She proceeded and probed his opening.

Noises gushed from him, the sounds more animal than human.

A wonderful response though not enough. Constance needed everything so these moments would console her through the empty and dark times ahead. She licked his shaft, luxuriating in its faint salty taste, and swirled her tongue over the head then flicked the bumpy skin in back.

His loud groan filled the room. He clasped her head to keep her close.

She wasn't going anywhere yet. After licking his most sensitive area, she eased his cock aside.

He loosened his hold. "Wait. Are you stopping? Why? Don't, please. What are you doing?"

So many questions when she hadn't much breath to respond. "Easy, Detective. I'm doing this." She lapped his sac and eased his right ball into her mouth.

"Aw, God." He gripped her head harder than earlier. "This is too — it's — damn — I — you —"

His explosive sigh obliterated whatever else he meant to blurt. Grunts and growls spoke for him now, revealing his delight.

He deserved more and she intended to give it. She stroked his anus and explored his ball with her tongue, loving its weight and warmth in her mouth. He babbled something she didn't understand and figured he didn't, either. He was too far gone to make sense. His cock bobbed against her cheek as if to say, "Me next. Me."

She'd take care of his shaft in time. At this point, she loved his nut good and long before releasing it so she could coax his other ball inside her mouth.

"Oh, hell, yeah." His coarse breaths came faster and harder. "Don't stop. Don't. I mean it. Don't."

She hadn't come close to pausing even once and wouldn't now. That would be mean. She patted his ass to assure him things were on track and would stay that way. Multitasking, she teased his anus lightly, worked his shaft hard and sucked his nut.

A bawdy sound escaped him, part groan, part bellow. He tugged her hair. "No, no, no. I'm going to come."

That was the idea.

He growled. "I can't."

She freed his ball. He'd clenched his jaw so much it must have hurt. His complexion was almost as dark as hers, his face bathed in perspiration. "Why not?"

"What?"

"Why can't you come?"

"Because." His shoulders heaved.

If he'd been a woman, she would have predicted he was about to bawl. "Because why?"

"How can you ask that?"

"Ask what?"

"What you are. What you did." He ground his teeth. "Don't you understand? I'm holding off."

"Yeah, I got that. But why, for God's sake?"

"I have to be inside you when I come." He trembled worse than a whipped dog. "I just have to."

"Hey, hey, hey, no problem." This was epic. No man had ever lost it to this degree with her. "I promise you will be when that happens."

She slipped his cock into her mouth. Technically, that gave him what he wanted.

He groaned loud enough to wake the neighbors and pressed closer.

Taking in his full length would be a challenge given his size, which was more than average. She wasn't daunted and opened her throat.

He held her head and pumped his hips gently in encouragement.

Little by little, they edged closer to each other. At last, her nose touched his fragrant pelt. She inhaled, adoring his musk.

He grunted. "More."

Ever obedient to their desires, she fondled his nuts and eased his cock in and out of her mouth, her tongue licking, stroking, tempting.

Gabe choked out a new noise, more primitive than the previous ones. He thrust his hips, trying to control the act.

Wasn't going to happen. This was her show. She trapped his crown between her lips and drew her tongue over his succulent flesh.

His knees bumped her shoulders and his balls constricted, possibly ready to shoot their load.

It was too damn soon. She wanted him to work for release and earn it. Determined to reach that outcome, she stilled.

He panted and shuddered. "What are you doing? Why'd you stop? Don't."

He'd deflated a bit. Not wanting that, she worked his cock fast and hard as she figured he liked.

"Oh, my fucking God."

She caressed his balls and stroked his anus.

An impressive howl tore from him.

His thick, velvety cum spurted into her mouth, the flavor slightly salty and totally awesome. She gripped his ass and enjoyed.

He shivered.

Once she'd drunk him dry, she licked his shaft and balls.

"Oh, fuck, no." He wiggled away. "It's too soon. Too much. Can't take it. Stop!"

She already had. "Easy." She opened her arms and invited him into her embrace.

Chest pumping, he dropped to his knees and rested his arms around her waist.

His weight and warmth provided safety and contentment she could get used to but would never know for longer than a few hours. Dismissing her futile longing, she restrained her powers and stroked his scalp. Now wasn't the time for him to forget this. That would come when she had no other choice. "Good?"

He grunted something.

Constance smiled. "Hmm, let me guess again. Was it bad?"

He pulled her into his embrace with far more strength than he should have had.

Color her impressed. "You're cocked and loaded again? Already?"

"Fucking A." He caught another breath. "On the bed."

Gabe figured the next minutes might kill him, but no damn way would he let on how pooped he was. He didn't want their relationship to begin on such a sorry note and needed to prove he had endurance to spare.

He struggled to his feet. His knees popped. The pain woke him, somewhat. Dizzy, he swayed.

Constance stood and reached out. "Are you all right?"

After a ten-minute nap, he'd be great, but would never admit it. "No. You're still not on the bed."

She raised her hands in surrender, padded toward it and stopped. "Wait."

"No." Her bouncing ass drove him crazy. "Why?"

She returned and swiped the cuffs from where he'd dropped them. "Might need these."

In his world, that was the one sure thing besides death and taxes. "Good idea. You're really on the ball."

"Make that balls and I will be."

He laughed even though it used too much energy.

Wearing a pleased smile, she backed to the bed, her muscles taut, her complexion flawless and dewy with youth.

His weary cock tried to defy gravity to point at her but wasn't hard enough yet. If the damn thing could have talked, it would have shouted, "Follow her, fool!"

Gabe did and stumbled, his pants and underwear bunched around his ankles. He windmilled his arms and righted himself.

Constance rested one knee on the mattress. "You okay?"

He'd never been better. What a vision she created, her hair dangling past her shoulders, lustrous as hell, one tress dipping over her eye, making her look like a femme fatale. Her nipples were dusky as he'd imagined. Boobs ripe and weighty, ass plush.

His balls perked up the same as when she'd sucked them. "I'm fine." He took another step in his clothes and twisted to keep from falling on his face.

She pressed her fingers to her mouth but didn't hide her smile. "You coming?"

She was a bad, bad girl, making light of him. How he'd lived without her this long, he wasn't sure.

He toed off his shoes, ditched his pants, boxer briefs and socks. With great care, he placed his holstered gun on the dresser well away from them. He was about to toss his tie aside but reconsidered. His handcuffs were too harsh to use on her, the tie more intimate. He pitched it toward the bed.

It dropped on her ankle. She arched one slender eyebrow.

Liking her sass, he pulled off his shirt, not bothering to undo the cuffs. The buttons flew across the room. One hit the chair.

"Whoa." She stroked her throat. "If you're not careful you'll ruin your clothes."

"Taking care isn't on my itinerary tonight. Or yours."

"No?" She drew her tongue across her lips.

He liked that.

"Guess I'll have to go along with the program then."

He loved when she talked dirty. "Good idea. So what's stopping you?"

She sank to the mattress, back arched, legs parted, showing him her goodies. Soft folds, puffy and slick with desire.

His fatigue was ancient history, his tool stiffening, though not as much as he would have liked. His only solution was to stall until he was fully charged. He left the room.

"Hey." The bedframe squeaked with her movements. "Where are you going?"

"Be right back. Don't move." He returned with two gooseneck lamps from his home office.

She regarded the bedroom ones already shining brightly.

Not enough for him. After setting up the others, he positioned both so they'd shine on her, hiding nothing.

Constance shielded her eyes with her hand. "Planning on grilling me, Detective?"

He fought a smile. "You have no idea."

"Why don't you show me?"

He swiped his tie and crawled across the mattress to her.

Before he got too close, she planted her foot on his groin and rubbed her toes over his cock.

Shocking pleasure coursed through him. He shivered.

She cooed. "Gonna tie me up?"

"Have to. You've been bad."

"The absolute worst." She held out her wrists. Playful as always. More beguiling than the law should have allowed.

Tenderness and something else Gabe couldn't identify raced through him. He wanted to hold and love her until the year ended and the new one had grown old. Controlling himself, he wrapped his tie around her wrists and eased her down to secure her to the headboard.

His cock swayed above her mouth.

She snaked out her tongue to lick him.

"Uh-uh." He shifted away. "Been there, done that."

"You only do things once and never again?"

With her, he'd repeat himself until he couldn't function any longer. "Let's see."

She pushed out her bottom lip. "That's no answer."

"How's this?" He latched onto her nipple.

A soft moan rushed from her.

Her skin tasted as rich as it looked, the faint saltiness a delight. He sucked harder.

She tugged her bonds. The headboard rattled.

He spoke around her nipple. "What's wrong?"

"I want to touch you."

"Now? You don't like this?"

She wrinkled her nose. "Of course, I do. It's hot. Why'd you stop?"

If he lived to a million, he'd never understand women. "Then we're good to go? Or do you want me to untie you?"

"Don't you dare. Why are you making this so difficult?"

"Didn't know I was. Forgive me?"

"Quit talking and get down to business and I might."

She was too good to him. He unfolded his length on her and swept his tongue over her nipple, making the long tip harder.

She arched her back, relinquishing herself to his passion.

The response he needed. He cupped her furry mound and lost what little breath he had. Her curls were extraordinarily soft, her cleft un-fucking-believable, damp as hell, the folds plumper than before.

He stroked her rigid clit.

She gasped.

Not wanting to rush her pleasure, he traced her cleft and showered attention on her other boob, sucking her nipple gently, hard then softly again, gauging what she enjoyed best.

Pleased noises flowed from her. She pushed closer, allowing everything he did.

There wasn't a greater gift a woman could give a man. Delighted, he indulged in his basest desires, using her nipple, tugging the delicate curls between her legs and returning to her clit. He stroked fast and hard.

She moaned lustily and lifted her hips, offering him greater access to what he had to have.

Gabe buried his face in her pussy. The finest suede wasn't softer than her folds. No fragrance on Earth matched her vibrant and exhilarating musk. His ears buzzed.

He worked two fingers into her hot, tight sheath, confining her for his use.

She parted her legs even more, not only allowing the intimacy, welcoming it.

Thrilled, he held her clit between his teeth and licked it relentlessly.

Her satisfied cries filled the room, adult music to stir the soul. She pressed her thighs against his head imprisoning him as he did her.

With dogged determination, he licked then halted but only when she sounded too near climax. Deliberately, he paused, letting her coming release drift away.

"No." She pounded her heels into the mattress. "Don't stop. You're driving me crazy."

That was his plan. He halted repeatedly and indulged in a few teasing strokes to drive her back to the precipice. Perspiration coated her. Her fragrance was richer, headier, scenting the bed and him.

It was time.

He swept his tongue over her clit without interruption, even after she cried out, announcing her peak. He gave her no rest, continuing to arouse.

She gasped and wailed delightedly.

Before she floated down from the most intense pleasure, he grabbed a condom and rolled the sucker on at supersonic speed. Once sheathed, he crawled between her legs.

Her lids were heavy, face flushed, lips parted.

He brushed his mouth over hers and positioned himself. "Ready?"

"God, yeah."

The best words ever. Smiling, he bathed his crown in her pussy, drenched from her desire, and drove himself deeply inside.

Chapter Six

Filled, Constance reveled in Gabe's size, the heat and raw sexuality radiating from him. She'd always liked big men. He didn't disappoint. His cock stretched her channel, demanding it accommodate him. A choice she gladly made. "Untie me."

Head lowered, he lifted his shoulders to his ears and shuddered. "What?"

He was enjoying himself too much to pay attention to mere words or her needs. She hated to be bitchy and tried to rein in her frustration. "Undo my wrists."

He didn't budge.

She yanked against the tie. Her hands snapped back, sending her knuckles into the slats. Pain shot straight to her teeth. She gasped.

He cradled her hands. "Hey, you all right?"

Her fingers hurt like a sonofabitch and she couldn't get loose. Of course, she wasn't okay. "I have to touch you, dammit. Untie this fucking thing right now. Please. Do. Not. Make. Me. Wait."

"Easy. I'm doing it. You tugged so hard the knot's really tight."

As he struggled with the damn thing, perspiration dripped from his chest to her boob. Constance strained to lick him dry. A neck muscle pulled. New agony tore through her. She clenched her teeth at the pain and breathed hard.

"I'm hurrying." He clawed and pulled on the knot.

The tie fell away.

"Thanks. You're a good man. The absolute best."

He chuckled. "I simply untied you."

Wrong. He filled her and also brimmed with desire that matched the emotions burgeoning through her heart clear to her soul. She cupped his beautiful face, captured his mouth and drove her tongue as deeply inside as he'd burrowed his cock into her cunt. Wrapped up in too much pleasure, she couldn't stop kissing him until her lungs ached for a full breath.

Gabe's eyes were glassy. His cock flexed within her sheath.

"Go on." She wiggled her groin against his. "Pump away."

He blinked and squinted like someone trying to focus. "You're sure?"

"Do whatever you want."

His chin hit his chest. Once he'd managed a strained breath, he regarded her. His irises were silvery in the intense light, his demeanor pure male, filled with hard need. "Ready?"

"Absolutely."

Grinning, he got down to business but didn't rush. His cock's slow slide within her pussy intensified the friction between them far more than if he'd pounded away. Her cunt tightened around his shaft. His rod got harder, thicker, too. She wasn't certain her channel could contain much more, though she'd try to do so until her dying breath. Wonderfully confined, completely vulnerable, she squeezed her inner muscles around his shaft.

His color deepened. He gulped air.

That proved her effect on him. She gave him a smug smile.

His was as conceited. He stroked her clit.

Too much pleasure sprinted through her, taking her breath away, making her shiver. She collapsed, a slave to desire.

Gabe touched his nose to hers. "Now who's boss?"

They both were, giving their all to bring each other mutual delight.

Constance gripped his biceps and pulled her legs back farther so he could sink his cock more deeply within her. Their curls touched. His balls tapped her ass.

With a pleased grin, he eased back and thrust inside, faster, harder too, using her expertly. They were so attuned to each other's rhythm she wasn't certain where she ended and he began. The bed frame groaned from his ardent thrusts. Her breasts shimmied.

Climax whispered close. She clung to Gabe, needing him to anchor her against inconceivable desire. Lust became her world. Release, her goal.

He slowed, spacing each pump, delaying pleasure.

Her promising orgasm drifted away. She wanted to smack him. "What are you doing?"

"This." He rubbed her clit faster and harder.

Staggering tension coiled within and built to an unimaginable level. She shattered and beat the bed in delight, too drunk from arousal to stop. Heated waves washed over her.

Rather than stop, he worked his magic without pause. She came again, twice to his zero. He was a damn machine, his endurance and willpower like nothing she'd ever experienced.

Sweat stung Gabe's eyes. He endured the discomfort and ran the penal code through his head so he wouldn't succumb to his intense needs as Constance had with hers. Poor baby was limp as a noodle, the same way he'd be once he blasted off. That couldn't happen for a long time. He'd give her the ride of her life, even if it shaved several years from his. No one needed to live until ninety, anyway.

His heart slammed into his throat and chest. His neck ached from clenching his jaw. Each time his boys slapped against her, pleasure and pain flooded him and warned he wouldn't be able to hold off much longer.

He wasn't about to succumb to that defeatist shit.

With his cock tunneled inside her sheath, he pushed to his knees and hauled her legs over his shoulders.

She blinked wildly and gave him a feral grin. "Where'd you learn to do this?"

"Police academy."

"Nice. I trust you were at the top of your class?"

"Graduated summa cum fucker."

She laughed. "Please tell me you have to take continuing education courses."

"Those are the best. Picked up lots of moves there, too."

"Show me."

He stroked her clit and pumped his shaft into her cunt.

Her eyes rolled into her head. She clawed air, similar to a drowning person needing to grab something. She clutched her silky mane.

Gabe had never seen anyone more beautiful. He used her intimately and well, driving his shaft inside and rubbing her nub. Enough to tempt but not to send her over the rainbow.

She scrunched her nose and touched her clit.

He pushed her hand away. "Keep misbehaving and I'll cuff you to the bed."

"Promises, promises."

He snickered, enjoying this, and liked her more than he'd guessed he would and that was a lot. She was so different from other woman he'd met. Feminine as hell, but easy to be with, like a pal. Or a treasure he'd never disappoint.

Calling on his iron will, he steeled himself against coming and glided in and out of her pussy. Her cunt swallowing his cock then releasing it had no equal. Her moisture glistening on him was the most amazing thing the world offered. He should have set up his smartphone to record this. Before their next date, he'd buy top-of-the-line video equipment to capture every moment. While they ate take out or pizza, they could watch their moves.

She squeezed her pussy around his rod.

His hair stood on end. He stilled.

"You doing okay?" She flexed her inner muscles.

He suspected she was trying to force him to pick up his pace. Wasn't going to happen. He'd show her who was boss in his bed. "Yep. You?"

"I'm great." She stroked his balls.

Delight shot to the top of his head then fell back down deluging him. "Holy hell." Breathless, he pulled her hand away.

She wiggled free and cupped his nuts. "How about we both win at this?"

Her suggestion was too tempting to dismiss. He was too desperate for release. "You're on." He went at her pussy and clit before she could go at his sac.

She gasped, coughed and caught up, fondling his boys as no other woman had before.

His orgasm crashed into him with the force of a semi falling from a hundred-story building. Nerve endings fired. If this was what having an out-of-body experience felt like, he was living the dream. He hit the crest, hovered for a moment in sexual nirvana then began his slow descent.

Constance writhed and moaned.

With less grace than he would have liked, he pulled her legs off his shoulders and collapsed on her. Their chests bumped with their labored breaths.

Rather than complain, she welcomed him within her sluggish embrace.

Intense well-being descended upon him, even though he couldn't pull in enough air. Dying was probably like this. Discomfort mingled with extraordinary pleasure.

Already wanting more, he fought sleep and kissed her throat, cheeks, eyebrows and mouth. Their tongues waltzed despite his fatigue and hers. His flaccid cock was another matter. It slipped from her cunt. After propping himself against the headboard, he gathered Constance in his arms.

She sucked his throat, her tongue tickling him.

He chuckled and smacked her ass playfully. "Stop it."

"No. I like something in my mouth at all times."

Gabe couldn't believe how lucky he'd been to find her. "How about this?" He leaned over and grabbed the beignets.

She made a blissful sound. "I forgot about dessert."

"No, you didn't." He held the bag from her reach. "We just had it. This is merely sugar and carbs to replace the fuel we burned."

"Did the server include the chocolate sauce?"

He rubbed his eyes so he could focus and opened the sack. "Yep."

"Gimme, please."

"In a sec. First, this." He positioned her against the headboard, legs spread.

She regarded him. "You want to make certain I eat while I'm sitting up? Afraid I might choke?"

"Among other things. Don't move." He scooted over.

She grabbed his biceps. "Where are you going?"

"You moved."

"So did you. Tell me. Where?"

"To take care of things." He gestured to the condom. "Now, behave."

To make certain she didn't start without him while he was gone, he brought the bag into the bathroom, ditched the condom, washed off as fast as he could and returned. "Damn, you moved again."

"Only my chest. I'm breathing."

And doing a fine job. Each expiration wiggled her boobs.

He lined up the pastries on her belly. Once he'd taken out the chocolate sauce, he upended the bag and sprinkled powdered sugar over the beignets and her curls.

She clapped. "Pretty."

"There's more." He opened the sauce container and ran the chocolate around her nipples. They constricted at his touch as they should. "Now we're ready to eat."

"Not so fast." She pushed his face away from her boob and wiggled her fingers at his spent cock "Gimme."

He knelt at her side and rested his shaft across her palm. "Promise you'll take care of it. Wait." He cradled his cock to his belly. "Are you properly licensed? Did the board certify you to do this?"

"Are you kidding? I invented the stupid board."

He matched her sly smile. "In that case…" He handed himself over. "Do your thing."

"I intend to." She dipped his crown into the sauce and smeared it over the column. "Now, we're ready to chow down."

Another standoff that they both won. "Whatever you say."

"Hmm?" She licked him clean.

He damn well let her. Acute heat and ecstatic satisfaction blended together to create an astonishing experience. She brought his rod back to life faster than mainlining Viagra could.

Straightened, she licked her lips. "Are you always this easy?"

"Only with you." He tongued sauce from her nipples and lapped powdered sugar from her curls. "You should see me with my perps."

She stiffened slightly.

He lifted his face.

Her smile was quick and wide.

It didn't mask the uncertainty and possible heartache flickering in her eyes. The alleged stuff going on at her office returned to haunt him. He hated that group loyalty or friendship might have pulled her into what could be a mega mess. "Everything okay?"

"Sure. I'm just hungry." She bit into a pastry, her mouth stuffed with the thing.

He guessed so she wouldn't have to answer personal questions.

They ate in silence and brushed crumbs from the bed and themselves. He'd wanted to suggest they eat dessert off each other but sensed she wasn't in a playful mood any longer.

"Let's take a nap." He gathered her in his arms. "I don't know about you, but I'm not as young as I used to be."

"Being fifty isn't so bad."

"What?"

She offered a wicked smile. "Sorry. Forty-five?"

"Okay, that's it. You need to learn some manners with your elders." He turned Constance over and paddled her.

She squealed and laughed. "Stop."

His hand stilled in midair. "For real?"

She buried her face in the sheets. "No. Go on. Do your thing."

"Yours, too."

"Yep." She wiggled her butt.

He spanked and tickled her until she couldn't take in enough air to make a sound. Happy, he eased her against him and rested against the headboard. "Just so you know, I'm thirty-two. I'd ask your age, but I know with women it's a sacred number, like their weight, never to be divulged to anyone even on threat of death, imprisonment or —"

"I just turned twenty-seven and I weigh one thirty-eight." She shrugged. "Probably one thirty-nine after the beignets."

He hugged her close, loving her curves. "The pastries were well worth it, along with the breakfast we're going to have. Right now, though, we both need to rest."

Before she could protest his plan, Gabe kissed her hard, held her close and slipped into a dreamless sleep.

Given her worry, Constance didn't expect to conk out, but did. When she awakened, she dressed Gabe's erection in a new rubber, straddled him and ran his sheathed cock down her cleft.

He rose to the occasion, literally and quickly. The man could have given lessons on how to please a woman.

Precisely what she didn't need, since she was falling fast and hard. The truth didn't stop her. After riding him for too little time and hoping it would never end, she came and so did he. They thrashed, gasped and grinned worse than fools.

Once he regained his strength, his tenderness receded, replaced by dominance. "Roll over." He planted his hands on his lean hips and look down his nose at her. "Go to all fours."

What authority. Her blood sang. "I like when you talk cop."

He snickered but sobered fast. "Assume the position."

She wagged her finger. "Someone's been watching too much porn. Good for you." She settled to her hands and knees, head lowered, ass raised, legs spread widely. A state that left her vulnerable and touched her in places too deep to imagine. "How's this work?"

He mumbled something unintelligible.

Good enough for her. "Don't make me wait."

Muttered oaths flew as he strove to put on the condom quickly enough.

"Hey, I was only fooling." She spoke as softly as she could. "Take your time. I'm not going anywhere." At least, not until sunrise.

Her heart cramped. She rejected the feeling and any emotion that didn't intensify these beloved moments.

"Damn."

"Everything okay?" She looked over.

His face was maroon. Shoulders tensed. Muscles bulging. He struggled to unroll the condom on his imposing girth. "Want me to help?"

"What? No." Sweat streamed down his cheeks and chest. He covered the last inch on his shaft. "Finally. Hang on."

"Like I said, I'm not going—"

He drove his rod into her sheath, straight to its hilt, and stole her words.

The others she knew vanished in a pleasured haze. Sounds became her sole means to communicate. She moaned in delight and grunted with abandon.

"Good, huh? I think so, too." He gripped her hips and rode her better than a cowboy on a bucking bronco.

The headboard smacked the wall. Proof they were doing this right. They abandoned whatever civilized niceties remained and went for the gold.

His roars and her gasps mingled to make a love song, striking in its power, humbling in its understanding of what a man and woman needed.

Still hauling in air, he peeled off the condom. "Give me a sec to get rid of this. Be right back." He rolled off the mattress and lurched across the room. Banging noises and thuds sounded from the bathroom.

"Are you okay?"

"Yeah. Dropped stuff. No biggie."

She liked his easygoing ways. Coupled with his other gifts, her falling in love with him was a foregone conclusion. She squeezed her eyes, lost more control but spoke softly so he couldn't hear. "Come back to me."

What the heroine in *Somewhere in Time* said to her lover.

Constance now knew how that poor old lady felt. Being apart from Gabe for a minute was excruciating. An eternity was looking worse than Hell ever had.

He staggered back into the room and doused every light but didn't speak. Neither did she. Wasn't necessary. There was comfort in their silence and heated embrace.

The next thing Constance knew, she awoke, not recalling having fallen asleep.

Light bled past the blinds.

Her stomach sank. She wanted to kill the sun, morning, this day and the others she'd face alone.

Gabe rolled over and pressed his mouth to her ear. "What's the matter?"

He knew her mood so well and easily, too, as if they were already entwined emotionally as well as physically.

She was a fool for thinking so. He'd probably noticed how stiff she was. Cops were whizzes at reading body language. Another problem, like his troubling memories she had to terminate as soon as she planted the fake ones. By next week, his moments beside her would be finished, with him no worse for the wear, while she'd be a hot mess.

There was no putting this off any longer. Now was the perfect time to act and get this over with. She faced him to touch his scalp.

Gabe caught her wrist and kissed it.

Her breath poured out, her resolve turning to dust.

"You sound hungry." He rubbed the curls between her legs.

He had no idea how deep her craving for him went, straight past her soul into her marrow. She would have liked to devour him for years on end. "Don't you have to go to work today?"

"In a couple of hours. What time can I come by your office this afternoon...if Becca allows it?"

He knew she'd have to say yes or have the priest hounding them forever with other cops, maybe the FBI. Constance had to settle the situation now but couldn't move.

He looked at her curiously. "What?"

She had no power against what was happening between them and was reluctant to fuck it up with new lies. Not that she had much choice. Torn, confused and scared, she rested her fingers on his chest. "Is four all right? Or would you prefer five?"

"Five sounds good."

For a mortal. For her, the doomsday clock ticked.

"We can catch an early dinner afterward, along with some jazz." He chucked her chin. "If you're willing to play hooky with me."

His enticing proposals were killing her. She had to put a stop to this now. "Okay."

After hugging and kissing her, he pushed up.

She did, too.

"No. Don't move."

"Again? You're getting awfully bossy."

"Sorry. This time it's for a good cause." He eased her back to the pillow and brushed her hair aside. "I'll call you when breakfast is ready."

"You're heading out to grab something from McDonald's?"

"And have to get dressed? Hell no."

She kissed his knuckles. "They deliver?"

"I doubt it. Even if they did, what they serve isn't close to breakfast. To me, it's a snack. I like real food."

Only the best for an amazing man. "Then that leaves one thing, you cooking. You can do that?"

"Last I looked I didn't need a license to feed myself or you."

"Are we talking jambalaya here? Promise me you'll follow the recipe this time." She shouldn't tease, it only increased their bond. Unfortunately, she couldn't help herself. "I'm kind of partial to my taste buds."

"Especially when you taste me." He wiggled his eyebrows. "This morning, I'll make simple food. Eggs, bacon, hash browns and toast."

He was beyond perfect. "I should help."

"Not a chance." He pecked her nose. "I like my ceiling food free."

She laughed and swatted his butt. "Go. Don't burn or break anything."

"If I do, I have nine-one-one on speed dial. You have my permission to use it." He pointed at his smartphone then waved over his shoulder to her, his ass cheeks bouncing.

When his footfalls faded, she buried her face in the sheets and wallowed in his scent. Her insides twisted at the impossibility of fixing this. Messing with his memories forever wasn't an option. Confessing everything would betray Becca and the others, not to mention blowing his mind. That would lead right back to eliminating everything he knew about the service and her.

If only there was another solution...

Struggling to find it, she fell asleep.

Gabe's impassioned kiss awakened her. He carried her to the table and settled her on his lap.

She couldn't allow it and pushed to her feet.

He didn't look pleased. "What are you doing?"

She turned and straddled him. "This is better."

"No shit. Closer, baby."

Eager to please them both, she nestled her pussy against his cock.

His chest expanded with his huge breath. He released it in a contented sigh. "Damn. You do know how to eat breakfast."

She clucked her tongue. "We both do."

They fed each other here as they had at the restaurant, though this was an X-rated version. She held a bacon strip in her mouth and offered him the other end. He ate it until their lips touched. They chewed fast, swallowed quickly and made out past the point of needing air.

She pulled in as much as she could. "We better be careful."

He glanced at their nudity and bods almost fused together. "I think it's a little late for that."

She collapsed in laughter and smacked his biceps. "That's not what I meant. If we keep kissing like we do, we might fall dead from not getting enough breath. Imagine the press reports when your force and my friends find us."

"Not to mention the crime scene photos on Facebook, Instagram, Twitter…"

"Hell, I forgot about that."

He rubbed her arm. "It won't be so bad. We'll be gone and at least we will have departed with a bang. Don't move."

"That again?"

"Please?"

Since he'd asked so nicely, she did her best not to attack him. "What are you planning to do?"

"Something we'll both like." He smeared butter and jelly on her nipples rather than on the toast and licked the spreads off her. "Good?"

"Oh, yeah. My turn." She slipped egg into his mouth and tongued the yolk from his bottom lip.

So it went until they finished the food and had to haul ass. Him to his job, Constance to her apartment.

Gabe offered to drive her.

"That's okay. I'll take a cab."

"Why? I can easily swing by your place before I go to my desk."

She didn't want him knowing where she lived, especially since she'd given him a fake last name. "Go on and shower. I'll call for a ride while you do. By the time you're finished, the cab will be here."

"We're not showering together?" He sounded like a child crushed to discover there was no Santa Claus.

She cradled his face. "Not this morning." That wasn't what she should have said considering there wouldn't be other times they'd soap up and love each other. Her already bleak mood nosedived.

While he was in the bathroom, she called a cab, dressed, paced and troubled over what to do next, not having a clue what that might be.

They kissed goodbye in his condo parking lot. He opened the cab door for her and insisted on paying with his credit card.

Tears stung her eyes. He was too good for her, especially since she'd have to keep fucking around with his memories to protect her friends. "That's okay, I have it. Put your plastic away."

He did so reluctantly and gave her a final hug. "See you at five."

Constance forced herself to nod and piled into the cab.

Gabe got smaller and smaller in the back window until she couldn't see him any longer. This was what her life would be like when he was out of it forever. She ached from the pending loss and had never felt lonelier.

On the ride to her apartment, she struggled over the right thing to do for him and the others, not bothering to put herself in the equation. Even though she had an endless need for him, her feelings weren't right. They'd never be practical. She had no idea how to make their relationship endure.

That didn't change her hopeful heart.

By the time the driver pulled up to her unit, she was busy texting Becca, Zoe, Heather and MJ with a message she hoped would keep the inevitable at bay a while longer.

Chapter Seven

When Constance arrived at From Crud to Stud, everyone was waiting for her in Becca's office.

Heather sat on the sofa. Hands clasped, she looked more distressed than usual. After shutting the door, Zoe blocked it. Smoke rose from her hair and shoulders, a sure sign she wasn't pleased. MJ looked amused, as she always did when the expected shit was about to hit the proverbial fan.

Becca leaned against her desk, arms crossed, mouth pressed into a thin line. She regarded Constance's hair, no longer hidden beneath a turban.

So sue her. Gabe liked to touch and smell her locks. Anything for her baby. A grin tugged at her mouth.

Becca remained grim. "I read your text."

Constance figured as much.

"You told him he could do what?"

"Wait a sec." MJ gave Constance an intrigued look. "You actually saw him again, huh? Like in, really seeing him?"

Did she ever. She managed a wan smile then focused on Becca. "I had to tell him it was okay to come here and check us out. He's not going to give up. Neither is the priest."

Zoe made a sound a rabid pit bull would have found intimidating.

Becca's frown deepened. "Do you hear that?"

She wasn't certain how she could have avoided the noise. Zoe was less than a yard away and still growling. "I know she's upset, but I didn't do this on purpose to piss her off or you, either."

"I'm sure you didn't. But I'm not talking about her." Becca uncrossed her arms and gestured to the door. "Don't you hear what's going on out there?"

Constance had grown so used to oaths flying and the guys manhandling clients, it had become background noise. The heavy grunts sounded like Stefin's. Most likely, he dragged a reluctant vamp, reaper, were, zombie or some other para down the hall. Although those poor jerks had signed up for the service, many had second thoughts when it came to doing the work.

Becca breathed hard. "Even though vamps don't show up until evening, we have clients all day long, remember?"

She did now. Being in Gabe's arms had screwed up her brain more than her powers ever could. "Can't we cancel the ones for today, at least until he's gone? If you're worried about losing the fees, I'll pay you back for them."

"Thank you." Heather sagged against the sofa. "I'm running a little short since I covered those two no-shows earlier in the week."

"You need to quit doing that." Becca's glare zipped from Heather back to Constance. "Have you forgotten the claw marks on the treatment room walls? What do you think a mortal detective is going to say about them?"

She sank to the sofa arm, and screwed up her courage to share the plan she'd failed to mention in her text. "I thought MJ could redecorate this place before he gets here. A makeover, like she did for Zoe."

"Keeps doing." MJ gestured to Zoe's coral pantsuit. "What she's wearing today is my design, too."

"No fooling? Wow, that outfit kicks serious ass." She'd wasted too many years being a genie. She could have given Donatella Versace a run for her money. "The cameo's a nice touch."

Zoe fingered the piece. "You don't think it's too old for me?"

"Absolutely not. It's elegant and —"

Becca cleared her throat. "You want us to redo this place for him?"

"Only to give him an illusion of a regular office with mortal staff."

"Whoa. Now you want to change everyone who works here too?"

She thought that was given. If they did nothing except alter the offices and treatment rooms, it'd simply be a thin veneer to cover what happened in this place. "Just until he leaves. Not forever. And not totally when it comes to you guys or the boys. Believe me, all of you are more perfect than I'll ever be."

"That's not true." Heather smiled sweetly. "You're beautiful. Do you mind if I ask you something?"

"Of course not." As a good fairy, Heather could never be mean.

"What would you want changed about me? I don't have wings like mortals think fairies should and I'm five-seven." She laughed softly. "Certainly not as petite as Tinkerbelle."

Constance rubbed Heather's back. "I know. But your clothes…"

She looked down. Today, she'd worn a white peasant blouse, white jeans, white belt and white shoes. "What's wrong with them?" She plucked at her top. "Did Daemon leave a food stain somewhere on me?"

"Nope." MJ snickered. "Try a hickey on your neck."

Heather slapped her hand over it and looked at Constance. "Do you want me to cover it with concealer?"

Given her current blush that was unnecessary. Her complexion and the mark blended. "Up to you, but you're going to have to wear something other than blinding white."

Her eyes rounded. "You expect me to put on my fetish wear for him?"

"No. Absolutely not." This was why her plan would never work. Regrettably, she still had to give it a try. "I was thinking more along the lines of what you have on now but in light pink or blue. I swear it won't be so bad."

Heather stared straight ahead, disquiet on her face.

Constance honed in on Zoe. "You'll have to stop your hair and shoulders from smoking."

"Like I haven't been trying?"

"I know and I appreciate your effort. Can you also, uh…"

"What? Make myself taller? Give myself bigger boobs? Get longer legs?"

"Ah, no. They're all fine." She forced herself to get the words out. "Your voice is a little rough." It sounded like she'd gargled with acid.

Zoe frowned. "Really?"

"Hey, I think it's great, but Gabe might notice."

She also stared, the same as Heather.

On that happy note, Constance turned to MJ. Today, she'd worn a snug tee and jeans rather than her usual Frederick's of Hollywood attire. She also sported bells on her wrists and ankles.

"Let me guess." MJ touched her bracelets. "You want me to lose the jewelry so he doesn't know I'm a genie."

"Not exactly. But you'll have to behave yourself."

"That's no fun."

"I know, but it'll only be for a little while."

"What about me?" Becca gestured to herself. "What do I have to change?"

"As far as I'm concerned, nothing. I love your look, but you might consider ditching the harem pants and top for a regular blouse and pants like mortal women wear in offices. Tone down the makeup, too. Just for this afternoon. It wouldn't hurt for everyone to look and act normal."

Becca shoved her bangs off her forehead. A few hairs pointed at the ceiling. "Define normal."

Anything that didn't happen in this place would have fit the bill. She gestured to Zoe. "In addition to no smoke rising from her and getting another voice, no flames should bob in her eyes, either."

Indignation filled Zoe's face. "Why not ask me to change sex, too?"

"That's not necessary."

"But everything else is? I don't think so. My guys like me the way I am."

"You're fine as you are. I'm not being critical. I simply want this to go smoothly and get it over with."

Becca pushed away from her desk. "What happens after we pass his inspection?"

If the gods were willing, dinner and jazz. Given Becca's scowl, Constance figured nothing good or romantic was going to happen unless she turned things around, which didn't seem possible. Her heart twisted and her spirits fell. "I know it's a lot to ask, and I wouldn't ordinarily, but I like him." So much affection and tenderness for Gabe rose up, she could barely contain her emotions. "When you guys were falling in love, I didn't try to keep you from it. I cheered you on."

Heather offered a sympathetic look. "It's true. She kept asking for details about Daemon and me…lots of them." Her face flushed a brighter red than it had earlier.

Zoe's color had risen, too. A tad more displeasure and she'd spontaneously combust. "We weren't involved with mortals."

"Well, duh." MJ rolled her eyes. "Most of them are so boring, except the ones I pick up. Don't you think?"

Zoe shuddered. "I never liked them."

"Maybe because you never gave them a chance, especially the boring ones." Heather clasped her hands even tighter. "I'm sure some are nice."

"Yeah, right." Zoe sniffed. "What about the SOB I sold my soul for? Did you forget about him?"

"Hold it." Becca crossed to Constance. "You're falling in love with him?"

She was afraid to say the words or let them enter her thoughts.

MJ smirked. "I'd say the love train has already left the station."

If Constance hadn't considered MJ and the others her BFFs, she would have smacked each for adding to her misery. "He's a good man. So what if he's mortal?"

"Where can this lead?" Becca gestured helplessly. "If this goes on and you guys get deeply involved, you'll eventually have to tell him the truth."

"Uh-uh." Zoe swatted at the smoke rising from her shoulders and hair. "I vote that choice down. The only thing she could do would be to screw with his memories."

MJ nodded. "Works for me."

Constance wasn't sure what to think.

Becca looked worried. "Have you ever played with anyone's memories repeatedly? Removing them and planting false ones and removing those and — well, you know."

"I haven't." She grew cold to the bone and wrapped her arms around herself. "It's never been necessary before."

"Then you don't know if it's safe."

She hadn't thought about that wrinkle, either. Her entire focus had been on getting through today.

"Sweetie." Becca cradled Constance's cheek. "If you want this guy, it's best he likes you for who you really are, not an image you're trying to project."

"I can't tell him the truth. He'll freak."

"And we won't?" Zoe's eyes widened.

Becca shot her a warning glance and regarded Constance. "If this is going to work between you two, you'll have to tell him sometime."

There was the rub. It couldn't turn out well, yet she had never wanted anything more than to be with him. "I don't know what to do."

MJ shrugged. "I say keep altering his memories. Could be fun to watch him go around in circles."

Constance bared her teeth.

Heather piped in, "If anything bad happens, I could try and heal him."

"With *try* being the operative word." Becca spoke to Constance. "Do you have your cell phone with you?"

She held her purse to her chest. "Why? I don't want to call Gabe and cancel. He won't take 'no' for an answer. Believe me, I've tried. And I don't want to give him up, either. Not until I absolutely have to. I need a little more time. Please."

"I'm not asking you to do either of those things. You need to call your mom and see what will happen to him if you continually fuck with his memories, with no one able to fix what you've done."

She couldn't stop trembling.

"Go on." Becca squeezed Constance's shoulder. "It's best to find out, especially if you don't want to hurt him."

She'd die first. "Will you just stop?"

"I'm sorry but I can't. You're racing headlong into shit so bad I don't know what to call it."

"I'm not talking about that. You keep saying him. It's not him, the mortal or the detective. He has a name. It's Gabe." She hated to act like a two-year-old but she couldn't help herself.

Becca nodded agreeably, the same as the others.

Constance wanted to hurl. She pulled her smartphone from her purse and pushed to her feet. "Everyone out. I don't want you guys to hear this."

No one left.

So much for getting some privacy. She turned her back to them and tapped the phone to call her mom.

The most respected voodoo priestess in the South, not a teacher as she'd told Gabe. That wasn't her only lie about her folks. Her father was a complete mystery. As far as she knew, he could be Obama or Michael Jordan.

"Hello?"

Constance wanted to cry. "Hey, Mama."

"My sweet baby." Her mom's unconditional love poured over the airwaves. "You sound worried. What's wrong?"

She needed to do a better job hiding her feelings. Not wanting anyone to overhear her anguish, she put distance between herself and them.

They followed. Heather even pushed off the sofa to join the group.

This kept getting worse. "Nothing's wrong. I have this unusual case."

Zoe snorted.

Constance glared at her. So did Becca.

"Unusual? How interesting." Her mom sounded delighted. "In what way?"

"Ah, I've already removed a few memories from this…um…client. Now I—or rather the client—wants me to plant false memories. I'll have to eventually remove them and possibly plant more while I'm also taking away the real ones. This could go on for a while. Weeks, months, possibly years." That is if everything worked out and she had a relationship with Gabe. She caught her breath and tensed. "Will it hurt him? Memory-wise, I mean."

"Is he mortal or immortal or somewhere in between?"

"Fully mortal."

"Oh, my. In that case, you'll fry his brain if you keep messing with it. Won't be pretty."

Her vision dimmed. At thirty-two, Gabe's future would be ashes, because of her. "What if Heather tried to heal him?"

"She'll probably start crying because she doesn't own the sheer force to undo what you will have done."

Constance's stomach knotted. "I've already altered his memories three times. Will the damage be permanent?"

"Doubtful. I wouldn't try for four, though. Is this client someone I should know about?"

"No. Thanks for the advice. Bye." She killed the call and shivered as she'd never done before.

Becca hugged her first, followed by the others. Even Zoe's heat couldn't warm Constance. Everyone swayed in place, making her dizzier.

"I have to give him up, don't I?" Her hope evaporated, replaced by heartache so deep she couldn't breathe. "I'm not going to have what you guys do. I'm always going to be alone. He's the one man I've wanted, who really seems to like me, and there's no possibility to have a relationship with him. We have no freaking future, because of who I am. I'm so damn screwed, aren't I?" She covered her face and wept.

Everyone stilled.

"This sucks." For once, MJ looked serious rather than flippant. "Why are we giving her a hard time? She merely asked us to change this place and ourselves to protect us when Gabe comes here. You heard her. He's not going to give up. We have to help her. She's always been there for us."

Constance hugged MJ for her kindness.

Zoe's smoke thinned and disappeared. "She did give my guys hell when she thought they'd ditched me for another babe in the second circle."

Heather brightened. "She offered to buy me lunch so I'd tell her about my first night with Daemon." Her face turned crimson. "I couldn't. I'm sorry. About this, too. What kind of a healer am I if I can't put Gabe's brain back together?"

"It's okay." Becca patted Heather's shoulder. "You're fine."

"We have to help her with this." MJ shot everyone a warning glance. "First with changing this place then with everything else. No excuses."

Becca looked torn but nodded.

Constance swiped away her tears. "You guys mean it?"

"Absolutely." MJ winked. "This'll be a piece of cake, as soon as I know how you guys want the place to look."

"Wait." Becca squeezed Constance's shoulder. "You will have to tell Gabe the truth eventually and risk everything. Are you willing to do so?"

"I won't expose any of you. He'll never know you're not mortal."

"What about you?" Becca regarded her. "Do you trust Gabe not to hurt you as a woman and as a voodoo priestess?"

When he learned about her powers, he'd wig out, but Constance knew deep inside he'd never deliberately harm her by exposing her secret. "Yeah. He's a good guy."

Becca spoke to the others. "Let's do it."

"First the treatment rooms." MJ took everyone in. "Anyone what to share their ideas for how they should look?"

Heather raised her hand. "Remove the claw marks and paint the walls white. The ceiling too, and the floor, unless..." She glanced at Constance. "Is that okay or do the rooms have to be another color like my clothes?"

"As long as the claw marks are gone..."

Zoe crossed her arms. "Why not paint them black? It'd hide every flaw."

Constance rubbed her forehead.

Zoe threw up her hands. "What?"

"Black's a little out there." MJ offered a brief smile. "How about I come up with something? Everyone trust my decorating sense?"

"Yes." They all spoke as one.

Several pops rang out. Three models for treatment rooms stood on Becca's desk. One had ornate furnishings, the same as the stuff in this office. Another was sleekly modern, perfect for today's shrink, yet stunning, too, as if Sigmund Freud had joined the fashion police. The third was utilitarian, a room one would see in a state hospital.

The second one with pale blue walls got the most votes.

"Now for you guys." MJ eyed Heather.

She leaned away. "Don't make it too horrible, please."

"I thought you trusted my taste."

"I do for when we're going to Whatever Goes."

"Anything Goes. How about this?" A faint pop sounded.

Heather wore a sky-blue peasant blouse, beige jeans and brown sandals, her hair done up in a ponytail.

"Not bad." Zoe gave the ensemble a thumbs-up.

Heather clutched her throat. "These colors are so gaudy. We're not even in a BDSM club. We're at work."

"It's only for tonight." MJ faced Becca.

She put distance between them.

Grinning, MJ followed, or rather stalked. "No reason to be scared."

"Easy for you to say. You were never called the *F* word in school."

"You'll still be beautiful after I get through. Now, hold still."

Before Becca could flee, a new pop filled the room. She stared at her black silk pantsuit. Completing her outfit were designer heels and a silver clip holding back her bob on the right side. Even her makeup was subdued, simple and refined.

Zoe frowned. "Didn't you dress me in that the other day?"

"Nope." MJ gave her a withering look. "I don't imitate, I innovate. Now you."

"Me? I like my pantsuit."

"You'll like this better." More pops.

Zoe's pale green dress in a simple A-line design radiated pure class. Her beige sling backs were another nice touch.

MJ circled her. "Now for your hair."

"What about it?" Her eyes goggled. "You're not going to make me bald so I don't smoke, are you?"

"There's a thought, but no."

"What about my shoulders?"

"You get to keep them, too." A new pop.

Zoe's hair was drawn back in a severe bun. "Hey." She clawed it. "This is so tight I can't feel my scalp."

"Sorry." MJ's smile said she wasn't. An additional pop had Zoe's hair hanging loose and smoking away. "Better?"

"Hardly." She massaged her head.

Constance hated to bring up the obvious since everyone was being so nice, but she had no choice.

"Can't you stop her hair from doing that? And her eyes are still flaming."

"No prob." MJ worked her magic.

Zoe blinked repeatedly. "What did you put in my eyes?"

"Colored contacts. They'll hide the flames."

Becca made a face. "What's with the cig?"

There was a lit cigarette between Zoe's index and middle finger.

MJ held up her hands. "I can't do anything about her belching smoke when she's upset. Hopefully, Gabe will think it's coming from her Virginia Slims."

"Against the regulations, but it'll have to do." Embarrassment flashed in Becca's eyes. "What about her...ah...the sulfur smell?"

"That's a problem now, too?" Zoe sniffed. "Is there nothing okay about me?"

"You're perfect." Constance meant it. "You're just not normal."

She wrinkled her nose. "I hear that's highly overrated."

"I wouldn't know. I'm not normal, either. I can't tell you how shitty my childhood was because of my special powers. Mama was always punishing me for trying to use them on the turds who were bullying me and the teachers who gave me crappy grades. If you think that was a cakewalk then—"

"Guys?" MJ lifted her hands. "Are we going to trade histories or get this show on the road?"

Constance regained her composure and stepped back. "Do your thing, please."

MJ spoke to Zoe. "Which do you prefer for a fragrance, flowers or spice?"

"Neither."

"Flowers it is."

At the heavy perfume smell, she coughed and wheezed in a breath.

Constance rubbed Zoe's back. "Breathe through your nose. It's easier."

"For you, maybe."

Given how she was gagging, her voice rasped more than usual. "Ah, MJ? About how she sounds?"

"Right."

This pop was so loud everyone flinched.

MJ pointed at Zoe. "Say something."

"Like what?" She gasped.

Constance covered her eyes. Zoe sounded like Minnie Mouse or someone who'd been sucking on helium.

"Change this now!" She flapped her hands, which made her seem even more like a cartoon character. "I sound ridiculous."

MJ tried like hell but the only range she could manage was the highest and lowest notes.

Becca rubbed her temple. "Leave her voice as is. We'll work around it. Oh, shit, I forgot."

Constance was afraid to ask but had to. "What?"

"We still have Stefin, Anatol and Taro to do. They'll have to smell like cologne and wear contacts, the same as Zoe, to hide the flames in their eyes."

"Totally doable." MJ gestured to the room models. "Are we agreed on the middle one?"

Everyone nodded.

"Hold on." Becca tapped her chin. "We need to tell the guys what we're doing before anything happens, and get the clients out of here so they don't wonder what's up. Zoe, handle your enforcers." Becca spoke to Heather. "Cancel all appointments until eight or so. Give those affected a discount for their next time here."

They nodded.

Becca gestured wildly. "Go."

Everyone hurried out except for Constance. Overwhelmed with gratitude, she could barely speak. "Thanks."

"Aw, sweetie." Becca hugged her. "I want you to be happy. I hope you find what you need with Gabe."

Constance prayed she'd have at least a little more time with him even as she feared she wouldn't.

A half hour before Gabe's stated arrival Becca herded the guys into her office. Anatol, Stefin and Taro kept squinting and blinking like they'd been caught in a sandstorm. Thankfully, the contacts subdued the flames in their eyes. Gabe wouldn't notice them unless he knew what to look for.

Daemon raised his hand as a schoolkid does with a teacher. "Can I ask a question?"

"Of course." Becca offered a patient smile. "Go on."

"Should I offer to show Gabe my feet to prove I'm no longer a satyr?"

Constance held back a whimper. No way were they going to pull this off.

Becca squeezed Constance's fingers. "Don't offer Gabe any information. In fact, once he's here, don't talk at all."

Anatol frowned. "Even if he speaks to us? You want us to be rude?"

"Not at all. Simply pretend you're busy with something. If you are, he won't bother you."

"Good idea." Stefin spoke to Taro and Anatol. "While he's here, we'll mount Zoe in the break room with me doing her first. Our delighted bellows will prove he shouldn't disturb us."

Constance wasn't certain whether to laugh or scream.

133

Becca slumped. "No sex of any kind while he's here and, even after he's gone, understand? This is a business, not a motel."

Daemon elbowed Stefin. "Don't show Gabe your cock, either. Heather warned me about doing so in polite company, especially when it comes to the pizza guy."

Anatol and Taro exchanged a glance.

The intercom buzzed. "Guys?" Heather. "Gabe's coming up the steps."

Constance gasped. "Oh, my God, we forgot about my office. Surely he'll want to see it."

Becca rushed to her door. "MJ! In here! Now!"

She hurried inside. Thankfully, the cut on her lavender pantsuit was decent. "What?"

"You have to fix my office." Constance figured it wouldn't help much but it was all she had. "Make it normal."

"The walls outside the treatment rooms, too." Becca wrung her hands. "Remove our slogan."

"You mean suppressing the beast?"

Constance frowned. "What else?"

MJ gestured in surrender. "Hey, just asking." Two faint pops sounded. "Done. Anything else?"

"Maybe some music." Constance tried to breathe but couldn't. "Normal office stuff. You know, elevator music."

MJ looked clueless. "Never heard of it. Is Elevator a band?"

"No." Constance bounced on her heels. "It's easy-listening music. No pounding bass. Just light instrumentals. Lots of violins and a piano piece or two."

"Ah, you mean boring and sappy. Like the Carpenters."

"Exactly."

Becca chewed her thumb. "And another recording to explain what the priest thought he'd heard to get him off our back."

Not a bad idea. "The regular music first, though."

"Your wish is my —"

The intercom buzzed. Heather whimpered. "He's on the landing."

Chapter Eight

Gabe didn't lower the door handle, uneasy as to what might happen once he was inside. If he detected anything illegal, he'd have to investigate, which would fuck up his connection with Constance.

He wasn't worried about her being involved in anything criminal. He knew her well enough already to know that wasn't who she was. However, she did work with friends, if her passionate defense of Becca and Heather was any indication. Messing with the people here would screw her livelihood and personal relationships. She'd have a hard time forgiving him for doing so, if she could manage at all. He wished Father Archambault had gone to the correct office in the first place. Of course, if he had done so, Gabe wouldn't have met her. The thought was too inconceivable. On a deep breath, he ventured inside.

Air-conditioning greeted him, along with the Carpenters' *Close to You*, one of his mom's faves. He tried to recall if schmaltzy music had played the last time he was here but couldn't.

Karen warbled away.

Heather wasn't as blinding white as Gabe recalled. Pink tinted her face and throat. The color grew redder by the second. She smiled so hard her mouth twitched. Must hurt like hell, given how she tensed her shoulders.

He kept his distance, hoping she'd relax. "Hi. Heather, right?"

She nodded vigorously. Her ponytail bobbed like mad.

"I'm Detective Legrand, remember?"

Another nod.

He hoped her reluctance to speak was because she was so shy, rather than being guilty about something she'd done. Thankfully, she wasn't hiding behind her chair as she had the first time he'd met her.

"Detective."

At the light, female voice, he looked over and couldn't believe how much Becca had changed. She looked great, normal, in fact.

Most likely because Constance had warned her to make a good second impression, and for everyone else to make nice with him from the get-go. He hoped that was because Constance enjoyed having him in her life and not for other reasons. "Ms. Salt."

"Becca, please." She offered her hand.

Karen finished her song. The tune started up again.

"Excuse me." Becca gave him a brief smile and called out, "MJ, the sound system is still messed up. Please fix it." She sighed tiredly. "If I have to listen to this one more time, I'll scream."

He chuckled. "No kidding. Hardly my fave."

We've Only Just Begun came on.

"Not much better." Becca rubbed her neck. "However, we like to keep things light and hopeful for our clients. I must admit, I was surprised when Constance told me what your priest said. If he'd only asked us, we could have cleared up his concerns immediately."

Loud hissing and howls floated down the hall.

Heather went deathly pale which provided more info than a confession. She'd heard the noises, too.

Becca remained serene.

Gabe didn't buy her act for a second. "Do you hear that?"

The howling grew louder. An electric guitar drowned it out, the ear-piercing twang followed by bass and thundering drums.

Becca ground her fist into her forehead and called out, "MJ, none of Jason's stuff. I told you to keep it light and hopeful." She spoke loudly to Gabe. "Her boyfriend, Jason, is the lead singer in Death Grip, an alternative band he just started. MJ likes to play their stuff here, hoping to get them some exposure. The hisses and howls make my teeth hurt. MJ!"

The racket stopped. Barry Manilow's *Weekend in New England* poured from the speakers.

Gabe's ears still rang.

Becca inhaled deeply. "As I was saying, Detective Legrand."

"Gabe."

She nodded. "Gabe. I'm guessing your priest heard Jason's latest. No wonder the poor man jumped to such a wild conclusion."

Sounded reasonable, yet the cop in Gabe told him it was a bit too pat, the same as her sudden change in clothing and makeup. "He's not my priest. He's a friend of my parents. Mind if I look around, have a chat with your people? What you're doing here fascinates me. I think it's wonderful you're helping so many guys who're having trouble with women. I know a few who might be interested in your services."

Wariness swept her face. She composed herself quickly. "Not at all. We're proud of our work. Let me show you around. This way."

Shuffling broke out, similar to numerous feet hightailing away. Possibly her staff ducking into their offices after having spied on him. Doors marched up both sides in the hall. One had to belong to Constance.

She appeared at the other end. Her off-the-shoulder gown hugged her curves. Its rose color complemented her satiny complexion. Gabe's knees sagged. She looked luscious enough to eat, right here and now.

Tenderness, desire and excitement sparkled in her eyes. She smiled.

He did, too.

Becca cleared her throat gently and spoke to Constance. "I was just showing Gabe around. Would you care to join us?"

She gave him her full attention. "If you don't mind."

If she'd asked him to crawl naked over hot coals studded with broken glass, he would have complied with a happy grin. "Not at all."

He reached for her hand and froze, remembering he was here on business.

Becca led them to the first room, rapped lightly on the door and opened it. The décor was tasteful and subdued, the guy standing next to the desk tall, bronze and blond. He'd dressed in full black and blinked repeatedly as one would if bothered by the bright overhead lights.

"Sorry to disturb you. This is Detective Legrand — Gabe." Becca gestured to him. "He was asking about our services."

"Actually, I'd like to talk to you about them." Gabe behaved as pleasantly as he could to the guy.

He looked wary and spoke to Becca. "Should I say I'm busy?"

Gabe didn't like how that sounded. "You mean to keep me from asking you questions? Why would you want to do that?"

"Our work here is confidential." Becca grew serious. "Because of our clients."

"That shouldn't be a problem." He talked to the man. "I don't want to know about them. Who are you?"

He approached. "Stefin here." He clasped his hands in front and lowered his head. "I came from a poor Russian village. Times were terrible — the poverty, the official corruption — you don't want to know." He sighed. "It's a miracle I survived as long as I — "

"Absolutely." Becca offered a strained smile. "Which is why Stefin's no longer there, but here instead."

Constance squeezed Stefin's brawny shoulder. "We're glad he is. He's helping our clients as we helped him."

He wore so much cologne Gabe could barely breathe. "You're his sponsors in this country?"

Becca and Constance traded a glance. "Of course." Becca beamed. "We like to help when we can."

Gabe gave Stefin a small smile. "How long have you been here?"

"On Earth?"

"Ah, no. At the service."

Understanding lit Stefin's face. "As compared to my life and after that, not long at all." He grinned. "My Zoe makes it seem like even less time. What a firecracker."

He'd lost Gabe. Constance and Becca were no help. They stared into space instead of interpreting what Stefin had said.

On his own, Gabe asked the most reasonable thing he could. "What do you do here?"

He puffed up. "I'm an enforcer. The best there is. You can tell Daemon so for me. He seems to think he's far better. All I can say is *ha*." He brought up his arm and made a fist. His bulging biceps strained his sleeve. The image on his hand looked like a stylized goat's head.

Either he was an animal lover or that was a prison tat. Confused, and a trifle uneasy, Gabe bumped Constance's arm. "Enforcer?"

Becca waved her hand. "A lot gets lost in translation. There are tons of rules and regulations in a business like this. Stefin helps to keep everything running smoothly."

"No one gets past me." He spoke through his teeth. "I dare them to even try."

Constance pressed her mouth to Gabe's ear. "He likes to think he's in charge. We humor him."

Her breath was impossibly warm and sweetly scented. Pleasure glided down his throat straight to his cock.

"Thanks for the chat, Stefin." Becca looked at Gabe expectantly. "That is, if you're through with him."

Prolonging this wasn't something he wanted to do. "Yeah, I'm good." He lifted his hand. "Nice meeting you."

"If anyone asks who the best enforcer is, you tell them it's me." He slammed his fist against his chest.

Becca closed the door and leaned against it, looking beyond wilted.

After having met strange Stefin, Gabe couldn't blame her.

She herded him to the next room, decorated similarly to the first. Inside was a pale young woman in a green dress. Two lit cigarettes rested on a plate. She held another between her fingers, despite the law against lighting up indoors.

Gabe squinted. What appeared to be smoke rose from her dark hair. He hoped she hadn't set herself on fire. "Are you okay?"

"Zoe's getting ready to quit again." Constance had spoken just loud enough for him to hear. "Every time she does, she goes overboard like this. We try not to notice."

She had to be pulling his leg. "I wasn't talking about the cigs. Can't you see her hair's smoking? I think she's about to burst into flame." He hurried inside.

Constance yanked him back. "Zoe, sweetie, your hair?"

She patted it. "I'm good."

Gabe recoiled. Her guttural voice reminded him of the kid in *The Exorcist* after the demon took possession. Her office reeked from a flowery perfume. Could be she was also from a poor Russian village like Stefin. That might explain why he'd called her his Zoe and they'd drenched themselves in fragrance.

"Zoe, this is Detective Gabe Legrand." Becca inclined her head to him. "He's here to check out our services."

Unwilling to put one toe back into Zoe's domain, he lifted his hand in greeting. "What do you do here?"

"She manages our customer engagement team. That's where Stefin works." Becca's smile was proud. "We couldn't operate the business without her."

Zoe blushed. "I do my best."

He leaned into Constance and spoke quietly. "What's wrong with her voice?"

"Smoking. Bronchitis. You name it."

"Better make sure she gives up the butts before she gets seriously ill or another cop comes in here and issues a citation."

"You're not going to do that, are you?"

"Of course not. But you better be careful."

She gave him a sultry look. "Are you certain you want that?"

His balls twitched.

"We'll let you get back to work." Becca closed Zoe's door.

In the break room, she introduced him to Anatol, a black guy with dreadlocks.

Anatol flashed a smile. "*Bonjour.*"

"Hi." Gabe suspected the business was sponsoring him, too. "What do you do here?"

"I'm the top enforcer."

"The hell you are." The guy next to him had spoken. He had auburn hair, blue eyes and a country accent thicker than the actors on *Nashville*. "You're just a regular ol' enforcer like Stefin, Daemon and me. Nothing special about you."

"Taro." Becca shook her head.

Anatol bowed slightly from the waist. "Thank you for coming to my defense against such a cretin."

"That's enough from you, too."

He sagged in his chair.

Gabe didn't get it. When he'd asked about the enforcer title in Stefin's office, Becca had claimed it was a lousy translation. Yet these guys used the same weird term.

"Looks like you just met Taro." She smiled weakly. "Rounding out this group is Daemon." She gestured to him.

He had shoulder-length brown hair and was as muscular as the other two. "Hey, Detective."

"Hi. You have quite a spread there for dinner." Numerous Hostess cupcakes, McDonald's Big Macs and Hershey candy bars.

Daemon glanced at his feast. "This is just a snack. I don't get dinner for another hour." He stuffed two Big Macs, three Hostess cupcakes, and four Hershey bars into his mouth. His cheeks puffed out like a chipmunk's.

No one seemed to notice how odd that was.

It'd take more than a few chews and swallows before he got everything down and could answer any questions. For some reason, Gabe's mischievous streak kicked in. "Are you always this hungry, Daemon?"

He swallowed his food without chewing, belched loudly and shot a guilty glance at Becca.

She gave him a disapproving look. "What did we tell you about that?"

He pulled in his shoulders. "Sorry." He spoke to Taro and Anatol. "People don't make noises in polite company."

They looked at him blankly.

Criminal masterminds these guys weren't. If anything, they had the same finesse as the Three Stooges. Throw Stefin in as a spare and Gabe figured Becca had her hands more than full. Either she had exceedingly low standards for employees or she was the nicest person he'd ever known for hiring this crew. A sane person would have run in the opposite direction.

No way could anything illegal be going down here...except for that enforcer term.

"Now, MJ." Becca directed him to the reception area.

Heather and a young woman jumped apart. They both held something behind themselves. A bra without cups swung into view. Something smacked on the floor. Heather swiped it up. Looked like leather panties, no crotch.

Gabe guessed they'd been gabbing about clothes, what little there was of the ones they held. The young woman, MJ, was built better than a nineteen-fifties pinup girl, though not as nice as Constance. Her tawny skin, amazing violet eyes, long dark hair and smoldering gaze made her perfect for adult films.

Maybe she did that in addition to working on the sound system and dating Jason from Death Grip.

"MJ." Constance gestured to him. "This is Detective Gabe Legrand."

"Well, hey there, Mr. Detective, sir." MJ approached, her hips swaying provocatively, bells on her bracelets tinkling. Her fragrance brought to mind incense, what an Arab sheik would burn as he fucked countless concubines.

Subtle MJ wasn't. Despite how sexy she came off, his nuts and rod weren't impressed. "Hi."

Constance gave MJ a hard stare. "Detective Legrand is here to check out the service and meet the people who work here. Our work and only our work fascinates him."

Sounded like Constance was jealous. What a nice surprise. As soon as they took off, he was going to reward her for protecting her territory.

He affected his hard-ass look and spoke to MJ. "What's your role here?"

"Whatever you wish."

Heather coughed and wheezed like she'd swallowed wrong. Becca and Constance frowned at MJ.

It seemed she was a bit of a nympho. Gabe had to set her straight. "An answer to my question will be sufficient."

"She's our intake person." Constance shot daggers at MJ. "She asks our clients about goals. What they can expect from the service."

MJ offered a feline smile. "I like to make wishes come true."

Gabe didn't nod. "Don't you mean dreams?"

She waved his comment away. "Let's not argue semantics. What are you hoping for?"

He wasn't about to get into his X-rated fantasies with her. "I think Constance can help me there." He cupped her elbow without thinking. The wise thing would have been to let go and act professional, but he didn't want to any longer. If the others here suspected he liked Constance or if she'd told them, he didn't care. "Where's your office? I'd like to see it."

"Good idea." Becca spoke to the others. "The rest of us need to get back to work. Now."

Heather hurried to her desk and stared at her computer screen. MJ offered him a playful wink and slipped into a small room off the reception area.

"This way." Constance laced her fingers through his.

She stopped outside her door, not knowing what MJ had done to her office. Deep down, she knew MJ had flirted with Gabe to keep his mind off the stuff really going down here, and Constance had played along, pretending to be jealous.

Okay, so maybe she hadn't faked much. Still, she trusted MJ to keep her hands off him. Given Gabe's reaction, he wasn't into her in the least. She couldn't have asked for a better response.

However, there was still MJ's weird sense of humor when it came to wishes. Constance prayed her office wasn't set up like a bedroom or a sultan's den. Holding her breath, she opened the door and stepped inside.

Gabe followed and whistled. "Wow."

She had the same antique furniture Becca did, along with numerous ferns, wall hangings depicting pastoral scenes and three Tiffany lamps. Their jeweled shades created a colorful kaleidoscope on the ceiling and polished wood surfaces. The room smelled lemony, as it would after maid service.

Constance warned herself not to gape or grin, since she was supposedly accustomed to this grandeur.

Gabe eyed her chair. A throne couldn't have been more ornate. "You must be important."

Appeared so, at least in MJ's vision. "I am Becca's assistant."

He turned a slow circle, taking everything in before he closed the door. "About that enforcer term..." His rich voice held a hint of suspicion.

She was surprised that word was the only thing he'd picked up on and forced herself to play it cool. "What about it? Stefin doesn't understand English as well as you and I do...or anyone else for that matter."

"He is an unusual guy. But Anatol used the same term."

"He's French. From France. Has a nice accent, don't you think?"

"I guess." He regarded her. "Taro used it, too. From the sound of it, he's from this country. I'm guessing Texas or thereabouts."

She didn't like where this was going. "What are you implying? That the term means something sinister? Like what your priest thought?"

"He's not my priest. And I'm not saying that at all."

"Then what exactly are you implying?"

He held up his hands. "Nothing. I'm trying to get you to look at this from my point of view, or even your own, for that matter. Don't you think enforcer is an unusual job title to use at a behavior adjustment service?"

Constance crossed her arms. "Did you ever think that everyone's trying to make things easier on Stefin? During his time in Russia, behavior adjustment usually meant the KGB, the gulag, stuff like that. He has trouble remembering customer engagement team. We. Humor. Him."

"Okay, okay. I get it. It's just that the people who work here…" He shook his head.

He had noticed other stuff. What mortal wouldn't? Her chest tightened from so much panic, she found it difficult to breathe. Just as quickly, outrage bubbled at what he was going to say or accuse them of. No matter how much she liked him, he couldn't trash her friends. Everyone had gone through so much trouble for her, including Heather, who felt like a prostitute if she wore anything but white here or black leather during her BDSM excursions. Zoe was drenched in perfume she loathed. She, Stefin, Anatol and Taro had to wear those stupid contacts despite how uncomfortable they were. Thankfully, everyone but Stefin had gotten used to them.

Constance tightened her arms, ready to rumble as Zoe always was. "What about them? First, our terminology doesn't please you and now our people don't, either? Go on. If you have something nasty to say about them, I want to hear it."

His eyebrows shot up. "Take it easy. I didn't mean anything bad." He shrugged. "Judgmental maybe, but not bad."

"What are you talking about?"

"Has Daemon been in an accident recently?"

She made a face. "No. Why?"

"It's just that…"

"What?"

Gabe waved his hand as one does when searching for the right thing to say. "Is he special?"

"Yeah, to Heather. He's her boyfriend."

Surprise registered on Gabe's face. "That hulk? Wow. They seem so different. I would never have guessed. Maybe I was mistaken about her being shy. The crotchless panties she was holding certainly weren't."

"What she likes to do off the clock is none of our business. And you've been wrong about everyone here." She'd never felt more protective. "If Father Archambault had stuck around and asked us questions rather than running to you, he would have known we're just ordinary people trying to get through the day."

"Ordinary? Are you serious? Have you ever talked to the rest of the crew?"

She struggled not to laugh and especially not to sigh. This was probably the way it would always be between them. Fitting together so well in his world, while hers gave him nothing but pause. "Admittedly, everyone here is slightly rough around the edges, but it makes them perfect for our clients. They don't intimidate those poor guys by being cool or sophisticated."

Gabe grew thoughtful and nodded. "Makes sense. Sorry for thinking poorly of Daemon. He seems so..."

"Guileless?"

"I was going to say clueless. Strange for a grown man. Have you ever watched him eat?"

"I try not to. Look, he grew up in an impoverished family. There wasn't enough food for everybody. As the youngest, he got scraps, if he was lucky, and had to eat them fast so his older siblings wouldn't take them away. That deprivation stayed with him. He gets edgy if he doesn't have food close by. I understand. Hell, I'd be the same way. Even if he's socially awkward, he's a good guy."

Gabe lifted his hands. "Not arguing with you at all. You work with great people. I'm glad. Thank you for letting me come here tonight."

"Then you don't think we're doing anything bad?"

"Nope. I admire your work and your colleagues."

His kindness and good heart were killing her. Helpless to resist his allure, she sagged against him and captured his mouth. Hours had passed since she'd last enjoyed his taste and scent. She couldn't deny herself a moment longer.

Gabe deepened their kiss and pulled her closer.

The world stopped and she came alive, her pulse throbbing, breath catching. Although they were as close as two people could be, it wasn't enough. She wanted to be inside his blood and soul.

Gabe broke free first. Breathing shallowly, he rested his forehead against hers. "When can you leave? Earlier, you said you'd play hooky with me, remember?"

She'd never forget. "I'll ask Becca if I can take off early."

"How about now? Not only asking her but also leaving for the day."

"You're through with your work?"

"I'm never done. When stuff happens, I have to take care of it. But, yeah, I wrapped up my cases as much as possible so I could have tonight free." He kissed her forehead, nose and each cheek. "Enjoy it with me. Every minute."

It was too tempting. She had to resist. "Okay."

Gabe grinned and kissed her hard. "I'll wait outside. How long do you think you'll be?"

"A few minutes."

"Thank Becca for me. She's a great person."

So many emotions welled in Constance, she could barely speak. "I know."

"See you in a few."

His footfalls faded in the hall and his voice drifted from the reception area.

"I'm taking off now. Night, Heather. Good seeing you again."

"You, too, Detective Legrand."

"Gabe, please."

"Of course, I'm so sorry. You said that earlier to everyone else. I should have remembered. I promise I will the next time. If there is one. Of course, there will be. You and Constance… Sorry, I shouldn't have said that. I don't know if she wants you to know what we know about you and —"

"It's okay. Bye."

The front door closed.

Constance sank to a chair.

Heather hurried in first, followed by Becca, Zoe and MJ.

"Oh, no, you look so sad." Heather held her fists to her chest. "This is my fault, isn't it? He saw my leather panties. I tried to hide them but—MJ and I should have been more careful. I'm so sorry." She hung her head. "That's why he didn't want to talk to me when he left, isn't it? He thinks I'm awful. I am. I'm—"

"You're fine, sweetie." Becca touched Constance's shoulder. "Everything all right?"

Zoe huffed. "Let's cut to the chase. Did he buy it?"

"He thinks everyone here is great." Constance sagged against the hard cushion. "He's glad I work with such wonderful people."

Zoe and MJ gave each other a high five. Heather wept happy tears.

Becca pulled a chair next to Constance. "What's wrong?"

Everything they'd done here today was a lie and they'd pulled it off beautifully. She should have been doing cartwheels in the hall rather than feeling so ashamed.

If she and Gabe did get more deeply involved, she'd have to tell him the truth, as Becca had warned. Assuming he didn't run away shrieking, there was no way he'd be able to trust her again.

From the moment they'd met, she'd done nothing except lie and evade, while he'd been totally up-front with her.

"Sweetie?" Becca squeezed Constance's knee.

She wanted to cry but didn't have the right. "Can I leave early? Actually now? Gabe wants to take me out to dinner."

"Of course." Becca hugged her. "Have fun."

After what she'd done and would continue to do, there was no way she could manage a good time.

Chapter Nine

Gabe greeted Constance with a huge grin she couldn't hope to match in her present mood. Tourists streamed by. Young and older women gave him the once-over and smiled at what they saw.

She couldn't blame them. If they knew Gabe a fraction as well as she did, they would be goners too.

He embraced her as though they'd been separated for decades rather than minutes yet kept his hands chastely on her back. Because he was a good guy while she was a damn fraud. Holding him, she pressed her cheek to his and forced back tears.

After easing away, he searched her face. "Something's wrong. What? Don't tell me Becca give you a hard time about leaving early."

"She didn't." Constance smiled as well as she could under the circumstances. "Actually, she said to enjoy."

"Then you should. She's your boss, after all."

"Also, one of my BFFs."

Gabe nodded. "I hope to see a lot more of her and the others in the future."

Wasn't possible. Constance's deception for herself was one thing, but for everyone else... She couldn't ask them to be something they weren't. It wasn't fair to anyone, especially Gabe.

He eased a tress behind her ear. "Why the long face? Tell me, please. Are you still upset about some of the things I said?"

"No." She rested her hand on his chest. "While you were here, a friend of mine left a message that she and her guy had broken up. She'd waited so long to meet someone like him and now she's alone again. I feel bad for her."

"Enough to want to comfort her tonight rather than play with me?"

Nothing would keep her from this evening. She cursed herself for not having come up with a better lie. "She has Häagen-Daz to do that, along with a stiff drink. She wants to sleep. I don't blame her."

"I hope she feels better soon. Are you hungry? Granted, it's early, but we can have drinks and listen to music before getting a table. I know this great out-of-the-way place with awesome jazz. At this time of day, they cater to retirees. Lots of Gershwin, Etta James, BB King, all the greats."

Constance adored his enthusiasm and wanted him endlessly when she shouldn't. She should have listened to Becca before falling so hard.

Disappointment swept his features. "Doesn't sound good?"

Paradise wouldn't have been better, though these moments wouldn't last. She couldn't predict how long it would be before she slipped up or totally lost it and confessed all. Possibly a few more days or weeks. If she were exceptional at dodging the truth, they might have months. Years weren't a consideration. "Sounds perfect." When it came to him, she was hopeless. "How do you know about so many great spots?"

"I'm a cop, baby." He snuggled his mouth against her ear. "It's my freaking job to make this city safe for fun." He sucked her lobe.

If she died this second, her life would have been well worth it. "You're the man."

Chuckling, he glanced up at the building. Surprise showed in his eyes.

MJ and Heather stood on the landing, watching them. If MJ grinned any harder, she'd break her face. Heather wore her usual full body blush, her eyes sparkling with happy tears.

Gabe gave them a good-natured smile and lifted his hand in farewell. "Have a good one."

"You will." MJ winked.

He pulled Constance close. "Seems she's sexy *and* shrewd."

"You think she's sexy?"

"Not like you."

He was doing it again, turning her inside out, making her forget this couldn't go on. "Where are you taking me?"

Gabe kissed her knuckles. "Every fucking place I can."

They shared tender kisses in Rambeau's bar in between her smoke on the water and his bourbon neat. The band played the first strains of Gershwin's *Rhapsody in Blue*. Boomers applauded vigorously then fell silent. The music took over and swelled, captivating everyone, thickening the blood.

Throughout the piece and others, Constance and Gabe regarded each other, lost in their own world, a smile in his eyes, naked longing filling her.

Rarely had she envied mortals more than she did tonight. Once they'd found the person who completed them, they had a real shot at happiness. Not perfect lives, surely. Everyone had their share of crap, but they also had someone to help them through the darkest points.

Constance wanted to pretend she was a regular woman, or that Gabe was a demon, maybe a warlock, their backgrounds similar, both on the same page. She smiled.

He matched her joy. "What?"

"This is nice."

"It'll get better once we have a table."

With an hour to kill before one became available, they ordered parmesan cheese gnudi to stave off hunger. She accepted a bite from him and bit his finger playfully.

"Hmm. Nice." His nostrils flared slightly. "Care to eat like we did this morning?"

She leaned forward on her bar stool and licked the seam between his lips. "Only if you promise to arrest anyone who says I'm too curvy."

"You?" Astonishment crossed his face. "Baby, they don't make figures like yours anymore. Where did you come from?"

If she told him a voodoo priestess and an unknown male donor who could have been Magic Johnson or Denzel Washington, he wouldn't have believed her. "A long line of big, beautiful women."

"Bull. Next to me, you're positively tiny."

Even gigolos didn't make comments as good as that and they were paid to do so. "Have you always liked women with my figure?"

"Nope. Only yours."

She didn't ever want to leave this place. "Your turn." She slipped a morsel into his mouth and chased it with her tongue.

They kissed through the next set.

An elbow rammed into her shoulder. Constance jerked away.

"Oh, sorry." An ancient guy smiled self-consciously at her and Gabe.

An equally old woman plodded up and tugged the man's sleeve. "Didn't I tell you to wear your glasses?" She gave Constance and Gabe an apologetic look. "He's very sorry for disturbing you two. Come on." She grabbed his hand and led him to their table.

Gabe pressed close. "You and I are never going to be like that."

Her heart caught. He'd practically said they'd be together forever. Somehow, she wouldn't have minded ending up like those other two if it meant she'd have a lifetime with him. Not that she could acknowledge that. "You mean you having to wear glasses?"

"No. You and I wearing the same shirts."

The couple did have on the exact cut and color. Like families who went to Disney World and dressed the same in case they got separated. "Maybe she should put a leash on him."

Gabe bit into a gnudi. "That's probably next. Hopefully, we'll be at our table before they have to trek back this way."

For a place off the beaten track, this one was immensely popular as dusk fell. There was standing room only at the bar, wall-to-wall patrons at the entrance and too many couples on the microscopic dance floor.

Gabe pushed the empty plate away and took Constance's hand. "Ready?"

"Did they call your name?"

"Nope." He left his stool. "To dance."

She held back. "There's no room."

"After I yell 'raid!' there will be."

She laughed. "Given the average age here, we'll have to wait an hour or two for the place to empty out."

"I don't mind." Longing flared in his eyes. "Come on."

He held her close, giving her what she'd missed all these years—undeniable intimacy and a sense she belonged to someone. They barely had enough space to sway without bumping into other couples, but it couldn't have been more perfect. Having him want and cherish her was the greatest aphrodisiac and fueled her desire.

Yielding to passion, she sucked Gabe's neck and relished his heat, taste and scent.

He stilled. "Are you giving me a hickey?"

She bit his neck gently and eased away. "Sorry."

"Don't be. I'll take a selfie later so I can brag to the guys."

Her loud laughter cut through the other noise.

The older couple next to them stared.

Snickering, she buried her face in Gabe's shoulder and feared she might cry. Her damn emotions were all over the place. Soon, she'd be certifiable. She clasped him tighter.

He pried her off him.

Disappointed, she kept her hands to herself. "Am I coming on too strong?"

"Not for me. But our table's ready. They just called my name."

Hand in hand, they followed the maître d', who wove past tables and patrons, avoiding a collision.

Constance wasn't as lucky. She bumped into someone who grabbed her wrist, the grip icy.

Startled, she came face-to-face with Quentin, a vamp she'd treated at the service.

He smiled. "I thought it was you."

Her appetizer threatened to come up. To her relief, he didn't sport fangs. However, he did glance past her. She suspected at Gabe. No way could she look at him and reveal her panic. "Hi."

She prayed Quentin would keep his big mouth shut and not reveal anything. "My table's ready. Have a great meal."

"I will since you helped me so much." He shoved his hand in Gabe's direction. "Hi, I'm Quentin."

"Gabe." He shook Quentin's frigid hand. Immediate surprise showed on Gabe's face.

"Nice to meet you, Gabe. Did Constance help you, too?"

The room tilted. She hung on to Gabe's arm to keep from falling.

"Help me?" He frowned before understanding lit his eyes. "You mean at the service?"

"Absolutely." Quentin grinned. "She changed everything by making me forget the crap in my head. Can't recall anything bad now, though I know it was there because of the bill I paid." He chuckled then grew serious. "Wiping out those memories was the best thing I ever did."

Gabe couldn't have looked more confused. He nodded politely.

Quentin spoke to her. "What are you taking from Gabe?"

She would have opted for this conversation, if it wouldn't have risked screwing up his brain and life. Quentin must have thought Gabe was immortal. She cursed herself for not considering such a complication. There were probably a million more she hadn't thought of. "I don't discuss anyone's private matters. It's not allowed."

Quentin looked embarrassed. "Right. Sorry. By the way, this is Tiffany, my date."

The young woman had a healthy tan. She had to be mortal. Quentin's dream had come true since he graduated from his treatments.

Constance and Gabe shook Tiffany's hand, which was warm, like someone who had blood flowing through them.

"Glad we ran into each other." Quentin grinned. "Have a good evening."

The walls seemed to close in.

After helping her with her chair, Gabe sank into his. Rather than study the menu, he regarded her. "I don't mean to pry, but what was Quentin talking about?"

Stuff no mortal would understand. "He had a lot of trauma from an old girlfriend. I helped him forget it. Must have worked since he's with Tiffany now."

"How?"

"How what? You mean him being with Tiffany?"

"No. How'd you make him forget stuff?"

Constance recalled an article she'd read a few months back. At the time, she'd thought it'd make a great cover if she needed one for a mortal's unanswerable questions. "Hypnosis. You can make people forget what they want to forget. It's kind of like giving them amnesia, if you know how to do it."

Looking intrigued, he leaned closer. "You're a therapist in addition to being Becca's assistant?"

"I do my best." The same thing Zoe had said earlier. "Wow, this all sounds so good." She focused on her menu rather than risk another glance at him and additional questions she might not be able to answer.

Gabe was eager to continue the conversation, fascinated at her performing hypnosis to make people forget stuff. He also wanted to know why Quentin thought she'd done the same with him. Strange. Then again... A recollection teased, trying to reveal itself.

A server stopped at their table. "Good evening. I'm Patrick. I'll be seeing to your meal this evening. Would either of you care for another drink while you decide what you'd like?"

Constance downed her booze and handed him the empty glass. "Please. Smoke on the water."

Gabe shook his head. "I'm good."

Patrick nodded and left.

She stared at her menu.

Quentin and Tiffany reached their table. Her golden complexion made him seem like a corpse in comparison. Gabe recalled how cold and clammy Quentin's hand had been, similar to muck beneath a plastic swimming pool after it had been on the ground all summer. He couldn't understand why Becca or the others hadn't suggested something to brighten the poor guy's coloring, unless he had a skin condition that precluded it.

Constance chewed her lower lip. Perspiration dotted her temples.

It was close in here but not hot. Nor had Gabe's previous dates troubled over entrées as she did. "Don't know what to get?"

She flinched.

"Hey, sorry." He touched her wrist. "Didn't mean to startle you."

"You didn't. I was really into the music."

The band had finished the previous set minutes ago and hadn't started the next.

A feeling or memory tried to surface but didn't. Disturbed by it and her odd mood, he warned himself to stop being a cop. His duty was to make this evening magical for her. "Let's have a good time. Deal?"

She pressed his knuckles to her cheek. "I'd love that." Her mouth quivered.

Her lingering sadness stumped him. He supposed she might be recalling Quentin's shitty past. Her joy had plummeted the moment they'd spoken. Gabe scooted closer and kissed her tenderly.

She relaxed and gave him a yearning smile.

That's the way he wanted to see her.

Patrick stopped at her side and delivered her drink. "What will we be having tonight?"

They ordered the lamb shank, grilled asparagus and twice-baked potatoes.

Once he departed, Gabe touched her nose with his. "What about dessert? Want to bring it to my place like the last time?"

She rested her fingertips on his lips. Her own parted on a quiet sigh. "We can bring it to mine."

"I'd like that."

With pleasure awaiting them, Gabe made quick work of his meal.

Constance picked at her food and barely followed his conversation unlike the other times they'd dined together.

Something was still wrong, and he wanted her to tell him so he could make it better. That's what cops and good guys were supposed to do. Neanderthal thinking, but he didn't care. Her happiness came first. He brushed her hair from her shoulder. "Don't you like the lamb? You want something else?"

She curled her fingers around his. "What do you suggest?"

His only answer was what had made her happiest last night. "The dessert and check so we can go to your place right now…if that's okay with you."

"Overdue, I'd say."

He told Patrick to bring the bill pronto and their banana cheesecake to go. Gabe squeezed her hand. "Won't be long now."

She kissed his knuckles. "No, it won't."

They had so little time, hours in fact. The incident at the restaurant convinced Constance to do the right thing and tell Gabe the truth, but only after she indulged herself during their final evening together.

Nestled against him, she opened her apartment door and flicked on the lights, showing him her taste in furnishings. Certainly not what MJ had come up with at the office.

Each cocktail and end table had glass or brass pots filled with incense sticks. Beaded curtains served as a partition between the hall and living room. Her sofa and chairs sported red velvet cushions. White sheepskin rugs covered the hardwood floors. Vintage lamps rounded out the décor. Crystal fringe in bold, bright colors, dangled from the satin-and-lace shades.

She closed and locked the door. "What do you think?"

Gabe took everything in. "This looks like you."

Yeah, it does. The real me. "You don't think it's weird?"

He gave her an odd frown. "Not at all. It's beautiful. Don't you like it?"

"I like you." She cupped his face. "Make love with me."

He held on to the condoms he'd bought on the way here but tossed their boxed dessert on the sofa. "For as long as you want."

Constance would have asked for a lifetime but knew she'd never be so lucky. She slipped her tongue inside his mouth. His faint bourbon taste was nice but no match for his marvelous heat and strength.

Gabe embraced her tighter than he had in the past. On some level, he might have known these would be their last moments together. After pulling his mouth free, he lifted the condoms. "Hold this."

Once she did, he swept her into his arms. "Where is it?"

She licked his Adam's apple. "Where is what?"

"Your bedroom. Unless you want to use the sofa, table, floor or tub—if you have one. I'm good with all of it, even a shower stall."

"The mattress is softest for someone your age."

Scowling, he dug his fingers into her ribs, tickling her. She shrieked and tried to squirm away.

He wouldn't allow it. "Where?"

"Through the beads, turn left and go through the next set of beads."

He pushed past both. The colorful glass clacked against the jambs. Moonlight bled through her lacy curtains to spill across the gold-and-black bedspread.

Gabe pressed his face into her neck. "I like this room even more."

"Does it look like me, too?"

"Nope. Looks like us."

The best answer ever. She kissed him deeply. He dove in, not giving her a chance to catch her breath. Fingers tugged, clothes flew. Naked, they fell on the bed.

The frame groaned. His growls muffled the noise. Like rutting animals, they went at each other, Constance on top at first before Gabe rolled her beneath him. Imprisoning her with his size and weight, he grabbed a condom.

She gripped his wrist. "Let me."

"Gladly."

She eased the slippery latex down his ginormous erection, stroking him as she did.

His cock stiffened exponentially. Grinning, he entered her in one powerful thrust, her channel made to shelter and satisfy his shaft. He sucked her neck and lingered there. Her skin stung. He was marking her with a hickey as she'd done with him. She couldn't have asked for better. To further stake his claim, he gave her a lover's bite on each nipple.

Not to be outdone, she dragged her nails down his torso to his ass and stroked his tight ring before concentrating on his balls.

Gabe pumped into her furiously, shaking the mattress. She matched him move for move. Her desire surpassed lust and fun to reach something much deeper. A bond not even their separation would break.

No matter how many years passed, she'd never forget him. He'd always be her first and only love.

A man she hadn't believed existed and who could never live in her world.

Their first orgasm arrived quicker than she wanted. Thankfully, they didn't surrender to fatigue. Using all her strength, she tried to roll Gabe over so he'd be beneath her. He was too heavy and big, not to mention intractable when he wanted to show her who was boss.

In her bed, he always would be.

At last he cooperated and lay spread-eagle, hers to do with as she willed. She eased off the condom and tossed it aside.

He watched its journey. "Good pitch."

"No kidding. I only missed the waste basket by a few yards."

"In my book, you're perfect."

If only she could be fully mortal. She would have sold her soul to accomplish that if other crap hadn't been attached. To hear Zoe tell it, Satan didn't play fair when it came to matters of the heart. That left Constance with nothing to offer Gabe tonight except her unending love. She straddled his gorgeous bod, her back to his front and unfolded herself over him. "Dinner is served."

His weary laughter filled the room, followed by sounds that betrayed how much they enjoyed each other's sex. For sheer beauty, their artless, indecent noises surpassed the music at the restaurant.

He licked and sucked her clit.

Lightheaded, Constance enjoyed his cock far more than she had the lamb. She tongued his balls for dessert, not wanting anything else.

They climaxed, limbs and arms entwined, exhausted to the point they could only haul in air.

Throughout the night, she woke and roused Gabe, unable to sate her need for him. Despite his exhaustion, he denied her nothing until they wore themselves out and collapsed.

Constance didn't sleep. Couldn't. Misery built with each passing minute and hour. After what seemed an eternity, dawn arrived.

The watery light illuminated his profile, firm jaw and rich mouth. His upper lip fluttered from his mild snores, urging her to kiss and wake him.

She resisted, needing a few more minutes before saying goodbye.

His snores went from quiet to loud. He flinched at the sound, glanced around and looked at her. Tenderness and delight flooded his features.

Her confession was going to kill her.

He cradled her cheek. "Hey."

"Hi." She kept her hands to herself and forced herself to be brave. There'd be no turning back now. From the moment he'd first stepped into the service, this outcome had been inevitable. "I have to tell you something."

His mood changed from relaxed to cautious. "What is it?" After sitting up, he held her hand in both of his.

She had no right to such comfort. Getting tough, she pulled free. "Before I say anything, I need your promise you'll never tell another soul what I told you. No one. I mean it."

His cop's mask was back, revealing nothing about his feelings. "Does this concern a crime...something you've seen going on at your office?"

He was back to that, despite his assurances that he'd believed the fantasy world she and the others had created, plus the countless lies she'd told him.

At any other time, she might have been angry that he was still worried about what Father Archambault had said. Instead, she smiled sadly. If a mortal crime were the problem this wouldn't be so devastating. She could manage a few years in jail. Being without him forever was going to destroy her. "No one's done anything wrong there, at least not in your world."

"You mean me being a cop?"

"I mean in your world period. You have no idea what I am."

He stared. "Huh? Wait. *What* you are?" His arched eyebrows almost touched his hairline. "Are you okay?"

"No, but there's no choice now."

"No choice for what? What are you talking about?"

"What I am."

He cupped her face. "Are you experiencing dizziness or nausea? Did you hit your head last night while we were messing around? I don't recall that happening, but I was so into what we were doing I might have missed something."

"You didn't." She left the bed and paced. "I didn't hit anything. And I'm not hallucinating or crazy. I'm trying to tell you the truth for once."

"About what?"

"Me."

He looked uncomfortable then horror filled his face. "Oh, hell. You lied about being married? Do you have kids, too?"

"Fuck no, on both counts." She paced faster, wringing her hands. "I'm...that is...you see...what I mean to say...I don't know how... Well, actually I do, however..." Shit, she couldn't get the right words out. Maybe because there weren't any, which left nothing except wrong ones.

He left the bed. "What are you trying to say?"

Constance stopped. "Before I tell you, I need your word you won't repeat what I say to anyone, ever."

"Sure." He lifted his shoulders. "Why not?"

She wanted to scream. "This isn't a game, Gabe. It's vital to me. The most important thing in my life. You have to promise not to repeat what I tell you and mean it."

"Oh, baby, I am taking you seriously and I give you my word to keep this between us." He reached for her.

She backed away.

He regarded the distance between them. "Do you want me to put my promise in writing?"

"Of course not."

"Then please tell me what's going on."

He didn't know what he was asking for and she was powerless to keep it from him any longer. "I'm not who you think I am. To begin with, I'm not Becca's assistant."

He nodded encouragingly, stopped and stepped back. "You're not lovers, are you?"

Constance laughed. "No. She's into Eric. I'm clearly into you." She gestured to the messy bed and the used condoms on the floor.

He smiled.

She didn't return it.

His pleasure died quickly, replaced by a somber look he'd worn when they first met. "If this is about you not being Becca's assistant and having another job title, I'm cool with it if you are."

"It's not about a title. It's about what I do at the service, which doesn't include hypnosis in any way, shape or form."

He grew wary. "Is what you do illegal?"

"That again? Don't you ever stop being a cop?"

"No!" he shouted as she had. "It's what I do."

"Don't I know. But you have to listen to me. Absolutely nothing illegal has happened at the service, at least not in *your* world."

He threw up his hands. "Great. If it's not illegal then what's the fucking problem? How bad can it be?"

"Very. At least in your world."

"Wait, hold it." He frowned. "What is this stuff you keep saying about my world? We're both in the same one."

"No, we're not. You're a mortal cop. I'm a voodoo priestess."

Chapter Ten

Speechless, Gabe stepped back and then he laughed.

He couldn't help himself. Constance's teasing had caught him so off-guard he'd expected her to admit to something pretty damn awful. Possibly having dated creepy Quentin and other clients to make them forget past girlfriends. However, this... She was playing with him and being bad to coax him into spanking her again.

He shook his finger at her. "Naughty, naughty, naughty." Still chuckling, he padded closer, ready to turn her over his knee.

She backed away, arms wrapped around her. Tears ran down her cheeks.

His amusement died in his throat. Queasiness rolled through him. She was either the greatest actress on Earth and liked to take a joke to the extreme, or she honestly believed this shit. "I don't understand."

"Of course, you don't. You're mortal."

That word again. It sent shivers down his spine. "What is this really about?"

"Exactly what I said before." She brushed her tears away. "I'm a voodoo priestess."

"Yeah, I heard that part. What's it mean? You attend conventions with other people, sort of like a Trekkie?"

Offense pinched her features. "I knew you wouldn't understand. Mortals never do."

Gabe's nausea worsened. He feared Constance might be mental. Maybe she'd suffered abuse as a child, had alternate personalities like that loon in *Split* and her alter egos were emerging now because she was stressed out at being with him. Could be she found great sex and happiness daunting, just as others couldn't take bad shit.

He risked a step toward her. "I'm trying to understand, really. But I'm not certain what you're talking about. Can you explain, at least a little?"

She lowered her face and breathed hard. "Remember Quentin?"

They'd met mere hours ago, far too soon for Gabe to have forgotten someone as weird as him. "Uh-huh."

"I didn't hypnotize Quentin as I told you. It was a lie. I removed his memories, actually obliterated them, so he'd never again think about the woman who'd dumped him and he could move on to mortal babes."

There it was for the fourth time, her using the term *mortal*, as though she was... The only term he could come up with was immortal. New laughter threatened at how absurd this was. However, his disquiet for her sanity grew. "How'd you manage to nuke his memories?"

She clenched her jaw. "Don't you dare make light of this."

"I'm not. I'm just asking a question. Poor choice of words, admittedly, but I want to know."

"I laid my hands on his head and used my powers, what else? Within a second, the memories he wanted gone went poof." She waved nonchalantly.

Gabe would have felt better if she'd told him about chanting a spell or using a potion, keeping this on an even more impossible or ridiculous level rather than where it seemed to be heading. Constance laying her hands on Quentin's head made Gabe uneasy for reasons he didn't understand. A memory pressed close and flitted away. "You're telling me you have supernatural powers?" Simply saying it sounded insane.

"It's who I am."

Or thought she was. Surely, there had to be a reasonable explanation. "Why are you telling me this now?"

Her eyes grew shiny. New tears flowed. "You had to know. We were getting so involved."

Were. As in past tense. Like maybe she was breaking up with him when they'd barely gotten started. Despair tore through Gabe, followed by white-hot anger. He frowned. "What do you take me for, the ultimate fool? Why are you really doing this? If you've suddenly decided you don't want to see me again, just say so. I'm a big boy. I'll accept your decision. Hell, I have no choice, no matter how I feel. I'll stay out of your life for good, all right? No need to put on this damn act for me."

She let out an agonized cry. "It's not an act. I'm not revealing any of this because I want you out of my life. I'm doing it because I'm falling for you, dammit. I've never wanted another man more."

His outrage drained away, replaced by frustration and renewed worry. "Baby, you do understand that nothing you're saying is possible, right? It's fun to pretend, but…"

"Do you remember how you got from the reception area to Becca's office the first day we met? Do you recall what we talked about in Becca's office before I kissed you? How about what happened on the landing after you left—that would be before I came out and pointed to After Dark again. Do you remember the guy you were talking to? It's my guess you don't."

She pulled in a breath. "When we were at Pasquets your memories started to return. How, I don't know. But they did, until I made them go away a second time. Any of this ringing a bell?"

He'd never forget them talking and laughing at Pasquets. She'd leaned into him and brushed her fingers over his head. He'd gone blank, like a computer turned off. When his mind rebooted, he couldn't recall what they'd been talking about. Although he couldn't dispute what had happened, her explanation was pissing impossible. "This is nuts."

"It's who I am."

He refused to believe it. "You hypnotized me while we were at the restaurant and at the office to make me forget. Just like you said you did with Quentin when we were at Rambeau's."

"If that's true, why would I have done so?"

"I don't know. You tell me."

"How, when it's not the truth? I wish what you're thinking changed everything to your worldview but it hasn't. I'm a—"

"No. Don't say it." He pointed at her. "I don't want to hear it."

Her chin quivered, but she pulled back her shoulders. "I know you don't. Why do you think I was so afraid to tell you? You can't ever repeat what I've said to anyone."

"Are you serious? You think I'd actually tell someone else about this loony conversation?"

"Of course, you wouldn't." She ran her finger beneath her nose. "It would be too abnormal in your world, wouldn't it?"

He clenched his fists. "It's not my goddamn fucking world. You're in it, too."

She shook her head. "Not in the way you want. I can see it now. Nothing would have ever changed your mind on this."

Gabe couldn't stop trembling, his patience at an end, his fury replacing it. "This fucking what?"

"What I am. I shouldn't have lied to you in the beginning, and I'm honestly sorry for it. But I'll never regret these last days we spent together. They were more wonderful than I could have imagined. Now they're over. It's time for you to return to your life, to people like you, and leave me to what I am."

"Dammit, you're a who, not a what!"

"Please leave. Now. Don't come back." She grabbed her gown and left the room. A door slammed down the hall, possibly the one for the bath.

Gabe followed then stopped, not knowing what he could say. A part of him clung to the notion that she'd put on a performance by claiming to be a… He couldn't even think the term. Deep inside, he was still worried about her mental state. Her believing nonsense he knew couldn't be real. Even Father Archambault wasn't into demon possession, exorcisms or other junk, and he was a freaking priest trained to believe in it.

What was happening to Constance had to be psychological with a little hypnotism thrown in. That would explain why he couldn't recall stuff from the first time they'd met.

As to what else she'd said…

He dressed hurriedly. Whether he should say goodbye, write a note or send a text wasn't something he pondered. Right now, he needed answers, not another confrontation.

At the front door, he considered what he couldn't say aloud. That it was okay to get help when needed. It'd make everything better. And that he'd find her the best shrink possible.

She was too precious to Gabe for him to do anything less.

Constance sat on the bathroom floor, her head in her hands.

The front door closed gently.

If she'd been Gabe, she would have raced from this place, relieved their relationship had ended.

She shouldn't have expected anything else. Hoping he'd accept her real identity had been a silly dream. She repelled him now or he thought she was nuts. Either way, he was history and she wanted to die.

For the longest time, she couldn't stop crying. When no tears remained, she was too weary to drag back to bed. Adele's *Rolling in the Deep* awakened her. Stiff from sleeping on the floor, she staggered to the living room and her smartphone.

The screen displayed Becca's photo.

No surprise. Constance had slept all morning and well into the afternoon. It was past time for her to be at work. She answered the call. "Hi. I can't come in today. Actually, I can't come in for a few days. I'm sorry."

"What's wrong? Why are you crying?"

New tears fell. "Sorry."

"No need to be. Did something happen with Gabe?"

"No — yes — oh, crap." She doubled over from misery. "I told him we wouldn't be seeing each other again. I couldn't keep lying. It wasn't right. Everything you said was true. This never could have worked out, so I told him…" She couldn't continue.

"Do you want me to come over?"

"No. I don't want to see anyone. I just need to be alone for a few days, please."

"Of course. I'll have Heather reschedule your appointments. No pressure. Take as many days as you want. If you need anything, call, please. We're here for you. We're your family."

"I wanted him to love me."

"Oh, sweetie, I know. I wish I could make this better for you."

Constance smiled. "None of your potions or spells, please."

Becca laughed softly. "I promise. Take care?"

She just wanted to sleep. "I will. Bye." She killed the call and made another. As she waited for it to connect, she sagged to the floor.

* * * *

Gabe rushed through his paperwork, worry gnawing him. By four in the afternoon, he was able to leave his desk and raced to the building where Constance worked. He stopped dead on the sidewalk and looked up.

The theme song from *The Exorcist* played in his mind. He recalled the priest standing beneath a streetlamp and staring at the room where the little girl was, her being crazy as shit, possessed by a demon.

This is fucking nuts.

Constance had been confused. Maybe her blood sugar had been too low. There had to be a reasonable explanation, and by God, he was going to beg or bully her coworkers into telling him what it was. Hopefully, she wasn't here yet and wouldn't be while he conducted his investigation.

He took the steps two at a time and mentally prepared himself to deal with the people inside. They were rough around the edges, as Constance had said. Nothing more. He took a deep breath, opened the door and was ready to tackle Heather if she tried to run away before answering his questions.

The reception area was empty. No music played. In fact, it was eerily quiet.

Maybe everyone was eating a late lunch in the break room.

A door creaked.

He stepped back toward the hall. No one was there. The sound might have come from the other side.

An unearthly howl shattered the silence.

His blood curdled. He forced himself to calm down. MJ was screwing around with the sound system again. Next, an electric guitar would twang followed by drums.

The howling persisted sans instruments.

A loud thud sounded.

The howl cut off.

Never in his life had Gabe heard music like that.

The front door opened.

A guy slipped inside. Despite the stifling heat, he wore a hoodie and kept his head down, hiding his features. He glanced at Heather's empty chair then looked at Gabe.

His breath caught. The guy resembled a walking skeleton, sallow skin stretched over prominent bones, the whites of his eyes yellow, the same as his fully bared teeth.

The hair on the back of Gabe's neck stood up. He stepped back.

Hurried footfalls rang in the hall. "The reaper's finally here."

Gabe spun around.

Stefin halted and grinned. "Detective Legrand — Gabe. Stefin here." He spoke to the skeleton. Or as he'd said, the reaper. "You're late, again. Come with me. No arguments."

He had a headlock on the guy, who tried to fight but didn't have enough bulk.

Stefin wiggled his eyebrows at Gabe. "You can see I'm the better enforcer. Be sure to tell Daemon so."

Flames flickered in Stefin's eyes.

Gabe's mouth hung open.

"What are you doing here?"

He flinched at Zoe's voice. It still sounded as if she'd gargled with Drāno. Smoke rose from her hair and shoulders, only this time she wasn't holding a cigarette. Nor did she have a lit one perched on either ear. Maybe her eyes caused the smoke, because she had flames in hers, too.

A sulfur stink, rather than fragrance, emanated from her, the same as it had from Stefin.

Gabe's heart jumped to his throat.

More footfalls sounded.

He turned.

Becca skidded to a stop. She was back to wearing her weird makeup and harem duds. Her attention sped from him to Zoe, Stefin, the skeleton and back. She mouthed something Gabe could've sworn was, "Oh, shit," then looked like she wanted to run.

He had the same thought.

Zoe blocked the front door, arms crossed over her chest, her irises consumed by bobbing flames.

Sweat poured down Gabe's face and stung his eyes. He blinked rapidly, hoping to clear his vision and banish the freak show he was seeing.

Someone grabbed his arm.

He jumped.

"Sorry." Becca released him. "Didn't mean to scare you."

Her eyes were as blue as Windex, no flames. Maybe he'd just had a hallucination. Could be the lamb he and Constance had eaten last night had been tainted with slow-acting LSD or something.

The skinny guy wailed and still looked like a corpse. The flames in Stefin's and Zoe's eyes bobbed. Smoke covered her hair.

Becca got in Gabe's line of sight. "Come with me."

"No." He backed away. That put him closer to Stefin.

Stefin waved his hand at her. "Do you want me to call Daemon, Taro and Anatol up here? While I take care of Detective Legrand—Gabe, they can handle the reaper."

Gabe lost it. "*The fucking what?*"

"Reaper." Becca regarded him calmly. "Exactly what you think the word means."

He'd fallen down the rabbit hole into a Stephen King nightmare. "You can't be serious."

"Please come with me. I swear, no one will hurt you. But we need to know you won't hurt us."

She couldn't have thought he'd shoot them. A bullet might not work if it wasn't made from silver. Except those were for werewolves. These people were... He hadn't a clue what they might be.

On rubbery legs, he followed Becca and stopped at an open door. Gone was the nice furniture he'd seen yesterday. In its place was a padded table with extensions for the arms. Leather straps hung from them. Another set dangled from the end where someone's feet would be. The equipment resembled what prisons used to execute the condemned by lethal injection. Given the long claw marks on the walls, whoever had been in here hadn't liked the accommodations.

Drenched in sweat, he shivered.

Becca looked over. "Do you like Constance?"

Not expecting the question, he didn't have a ready answer except for the truth. He'd never met any woman he enjoyed as much or felt as comfortable around, as though he'd known her his entire life. If she hadn't dumped her voodoo priestess shit on him, he would have whizzed right past liking her straight into unending love.

"Does your silence mean you don't anymore?"

He couldn't stop shaking. "Is she here?"

"She's taking a few days off. Please answer my question."

"I do like her." His voice sounded worse than Zoe's. He cleared his throat. "But she said...and this...him..." Gabe gestured to the reception area where he'd last seen the skeleton and Stefin. "Them..."

"Would you like an explanation?"

"Do you have one that makes sense?"

"Not in your world."

Not those damn words again. He clenched his teeth so hard they ached. "Don't play me."

She made a face. "I'm not. I'm trying to tell you what I assume Constance already has. However, I'm sure she didn't divulge everything, in an effort to protect the rest of us. That's the kind of person she is."

"We all are," Zoe spoke from the hall.

Stefin, Anatol, Taro, Daemon, Heather and MJ flanked her, arms crossed over their chests, frowns dead serious. Except for Heather, who looked ready to burst into tears.

"Don't you dare try to hurt Constance or us." Zoe glowered. "If you do, I promise, you'll regret it."

He had no doubt.

Becca held up her hand. "Let me talk to him first."

Gabe didn't like how that sounded. "If our conversation doesn't go well because I don't believe what you say, what then?"

"You don't want to find out." MJ gave him a sultry smile.

He kept his attention on her and the others as he backed into Becca's office.

She closed the door.

Gabe flinched at the noise.

"Easy." She gestured to her sofa. "Have a seat."

He sagged against the wall. "Am I having a hallucination? If I am, please call nine-one-one for help."

She smiled briefly. "No hallucination. You're mortal. We're supernatural. Now, you know."

"Know fucking *what*?"

Something hit the door.

Gabe jerked away from it.

A growl came from the other side. "Is he threatening you?"

"I'm fine, Zoe." Becca spoke quietly. "Please tell everyone to go back to work."

Muted sobs filled the silence.

Becca wilted. "Heather, everything's all right." She spoke to him. "You better keep your voice down, unless you want Stefin, Taro and Anatol to ram their way in here, or worse, use their powers to get inside. Trust me, they don't play around, and no bullet is going to stop them. They're not alive any longer. They. Are. Demons."

Gabe backed away. "Please tell me you're kidding."

"I'm not. However, you have nothing to be afraid of if you don't threaten us."

"Threaten you? If they're d-d-d—" He couldn't even say it. "If they're not human—"

"The word is mortal. They're as human as you, probably more so. They've been through a lot of shit, and all of them are nice people."

"Sure. The kind who possess the rest of us, like little girls. Ever see *The Exorcist* and its many sequels?"

"This isn't a Hollywood movie. It's real life."

Gabe laughed. It sounded hysterical. "You've got to be kidding."

She didn't crack a smile. "Our kind has always been around, and I'm not talking Salem witch trials, the Spanish Inquisition or any of the other crap peppering history. Those incidents were totally bogus. The only ones who died during the scourges were mortal, because others, like you, simply hadn't noticed the real supernaturals right next door. All of you are too into yourselves. Selfish. Egotistical. Judgmental. Bigoted. Narrow mind—"

"I get it, okay?" He gestured wildly. "None of this makes sense. What is this place, a way station for otherworldly creatures?"

"The correct terms are demon, reaper, werewolf—were for short—vampire or vamp, shifter, warlock, good fairies like Heather who can heal, genies like MJ who grant wishes and satyrs like Daemon who are hungry all the time for food and other stuff."

"What other stuff?" Gabe prayed she didn't mean human flesh.

"Sex, okay?"

"Thank God. Wait." He pointed his finger at her. "I know what a satyr looks like. I saw *Legend* when I was a kid. Daemon does not have hooves, horns or a tail."

"He came to our service to get rid of his so he could look totally human and try to behave like one. The same as the vamps, weres and others who want to suppress their beasts. They're tired of being targeted by your kind. Besides, they'd like to go out with mortal babes for a change."

This was too fucked up to believe. "Mortal babes like you?"

She flicked her hand dismissively. "I'm half-witch, half-mortal."

In her world, that probably made sense. He inclined his head to the photos on her cabinet. "Is that your guy?"

"Yeah. And before you ask, he's a minor god, a direct descendant of Cupid."

Gabe should have been surprised but wasn't.

Becca smiled lovingly at the pictures then gave him a frosty look. "We're not committing any crimes here. We're helping people like us to realize their full potential in a mortal world. No one asks to be a were, vamp, demon or reaper any more than you asked to be born looking as you do. Tell me, Detective, what was it like growing up caught between two cultures, or worlds, so to speak? It wasn't easy, was it? Bet you had to fight a lot because of your blue eyes. Your lighter complexion probably gave you no end of problems, didn't it?"

His childhood and adolescence hadn't been a trip to Disneyland that was for sure. At times, he'd felt scorned by the blacks and the whites, neither group accepting him because he was different from them.

His anger and worry drained away, leaving him tired and confused. "There's no other explanation for this except for it being real? Constance is truly a voodoo priestess, just as she told me?"

"She's a wonderful woman. You're lucky to have known her."

Another female using the past tense with him. "Yeah, I am fortunate to know her. She said she could remove memories by touching someone's head. True?"

"She did it to you several times to protect us…at least until her mom warned about turning your brain to mush. Mortals can't take as much of her power as a supernatural can. We all pitched in and changed this place to make it acceptable for your visit because Constance was afraid to remove even one additional memory and take a chance on hurting you. She put herself and us at risk to avoid it."

He couldn't have been more stunned. "She did that for me?"

"Why the surprise? The only reason she didn't tell you the truth right away was because she didn't want to lose you. I've never seen her as happy with another man. I'd say she's falling in love with you, if she isn't there already." Becca got in his face. "How do you feel about her?"

He'd never wanted a woman as he did her, but there was this. How was he supposed to reconcile it with everything he'd ever believed in? "I don't know."

"Sure you do. Just say it."

"All right. I'm conflicted."

She looked angry and disappointed. "You're not going to hurt her by revealing who she is, are you?"

"Hell no. I'd cut off my balls first. I'd cut off any guy's nuts who tried to harm her."

"Good. Get on with your life then and let Constance continue with hers, please. I love her for who she is, even if you can't. She deserves a man who won't care about any of this, because he wants her precisely as she is and isn't conflicted by it."

After Becca's speech, there was no talking to her or the others. The guys escorted him to the landing. Zoe slammed the door and locked it for good measure.

Gabe shuddered, not knowing what to do. Dating a woman like Constance, possibly falling for her more than he already had and building a future with her, defeated him. He had no delusions what their life together would be like.

While he fought ordinary crime, she'd be here helping creepy critters suppress their beasts so they could date mortals. Like Quentin had with his young woman. Given his bloodless complexion and icy hands, he had to be a vamp. Gabe wondered if his girlfriend knew about it. Could be she was so into *Twilight* and its pasty hero, she found Quentin super-hot rather than freaking weird.

Gabe dragged down the steps, not understanding when the world had changed, making him the bigot.

He wasn't asking for much here, simply for Constance to be like everyone else and have the usual problems—buried in credit card debt, bitchy from PMS, into *The Real Housewives of Atlanta,* no matter how dumb the program was. To have her involved in something as fucking bizarre as this was nearly impossible to accept.

This morning, he had thought her strange behavior was multiple personalities and the end of the world. Now it looked like a damn gift. At least it would have been solvable with intense therapy and meds. This wasn't fixable at all. It was real, not a Hollywood movie plot, as Becca had stated. It was also forever.

And who she was.

He stopped on the sidewalk.

The crowd brushed past. A few guys gave him the finger for being in their way.

Gabe couldn't move and didn't know where to go. There wasn't a soul he could ever talk to about this. One wrong word from him would risk Constance and the others' safety.

He didn't want to imagine the fallout if the public had proof witches, weres, vamps and other paranormal creatures existed. If the various religions didn't burn them at the stake to whip up their congregations and haul in more donations, then the FBI, CIA or another governmental entity would confine and study them as they would lab rats. There'd probably be a constitutional amendment saying it was all right to harness a demon's or vamp's powers, without compensation, of course. After all, America had a right to confiscate assets when her protection was at stake. There were so many enemies out there, especially the ones with oil or other resources in their backyards.

The popular thinking would be to deny the supernaturals a right to anything. Politicians would argue they weren't real citizens, even if they paid taxes, and weren't allowed the same freedom and happiness as everyone else.

Savvy entrepreneurs might build zoos to house them and charge the public exorbitant admission fees for daily viewings. No one would consider it a problem since the creatures weren't really people. They were commodities, perfect for exploitation, or convenient scapegoats used to explain away the next war, Wall Street crash or tanking economy.

He never should have pursued this. Thinking back, he understood what a chance Constance had taken by even speaking with him, much less having done as much as they had. It wasn't as if she couldn't have had fun, removed his memories and moved on. Except she couldn't work her magic on him again without hurting his brain, and she'd already risked so much to avoid it. Becca and the others had, too, letting him leave without pulverizing or vaporizing him. Gabe figured Zoe would have loved to do both, but here he was, safe on the sidewalk.

Becca had trusted him not to hurt them, asking only one thing — for him not to harm Constance in return.

He couldn't ever. She was a miracle he hadn't known existed, and she deserved the best life had to offer — a man who accepted her as she was, who celebrated her uniqueness rather than wanting her to change.

She shouldn't for any guy, especially him.

His smartphone rang shrilly.

He flinched then slumped at the display. Nathan calling, not Constance. Never Constance. She didn't even have his number. They hadn't gotten that far in their relationship and wouldn't now. She had a right to be happy and to continue with her life, as Becca had said he should do with his.

"Hey." He tried not to sound too depressed. "I was just heading back."

"Make it fast. We got a new case."

More work he didn't want to do.

Nathan shared the particulars.

Gabe tried to focus, but he kept drifting to what he'd had with Constance. What he couldn't and shouldn't want now.

Chapter Eleven

Iona Queen, Constance's mom, lifted the pitcher. "More tea?"

Constance would have killed for a slug of bourbon chased by a fifth of vodka. Knowing her mother's distaste for binge drinking in the house, she shook her head.

"Sure?"

"Thanks, but I'm good."

"You're wasting away to nothing. You haven't eaten in days."

No appetite or energy. It was an effort for her to lie sprawled on her mom's sofa. At this point, chewing and swallowing were beyond Constance's capabilities. Yet another TV game show played. Six trillion cable channels and all they offered was crappy sports, foreign language stations and reality junk.

If only she could sleep. As tired as Constance was, she couldn't rest. Instead, she slogged through each day like a real zombie, not those fake ones on *The Walking*

Dead. Too many memories tempted and taunted her, the past gone never to return.

She'd considered asking her mom to remove every trace of Gabe from her brain but couldn't bring herself to do so. Despite how they'd ended, she didn't want to forget the magic between them. It had been more real and deep than she'd experienced with any man. Feelings like that didn't come along often, or at least they hadn't for her. To lose them after having waited so many lonely years was unthinkable.

If only she and Gabe had been on the same side, they might have had a fighting chance.

Now, though... The look on his face when she'd revealed what she was told her everything she needed to know. He wanted a normal woman, not someone like her.

Tears clouded her vision. She pushed them back, refusing to allow any more grief. She'd been here for nearly a week. Time to pull on her big-girl panties and get her life together. As soon as she could find the strength.

Her mom regarded her.

Constance pretended not to notice.

The silence between them became excruciating. Her mom released a displeased sigh and pulled back the lace curtains. Sun flooded the living room.

The stinking rays drilled through Constance's eyes like a laser beam. No wonder vamps hated daylight. She bared her teeth.

"You should go outside and get some fresh air." Her mom gestured to the front window. "It's a beautiful day."

It was no different from the others Constance had barely survived. She was still alone and hurting. "I should leave before I eat up all my vacation time. I need to get back to work." She didn't move.

"Becca called again this morning. She and the others want to know how you are."

"I'm fine."

"You need to tell her and them, not me. Why won't you talk to anyone?"

Their intrusive sympathy made her feel like a loser. Once she returned to work, everyone would be cautious around her, afraid she might cry or fall apart like Heather always did. Daemon and the Unholy Trio would behave themselves for a while, not groping or screwing Heather and Zoe in the office. MJ would probably suggest a makeover. Becca would offer advice, her crappy spells and a fix-up with Farron.

Constance couldn't face that yet or ever. "When they call again, tell them I'm all right. I'll be back soon. Tomorrow. Maybe the next day." Surely, when she'd used all her earned time off.

The front bell ding-dong-dinged.

Her mom looked over. "Maybe you should tell them yourself. That's probably them now."

Constance draped her arm over her eyes, praying the caller was unknown and hopefully selling religion. Those guys bugged the hell out of her mom, who lectured them while they tried to convert her. It'd be another Mexican standoff, leaving Constance in peace. "If it's Becca or the others, please tell them I'm in bed."

"After they came all the way out here?"

Constance held back a groan. "We're still in the French Quarter, Mama. I could walk from your house to the office."

"So can they."

Given the persistent ringing and knocking on the door, they'd done so and weren't happy about it. "I don't want to see anyone."

"Maybe not, but it will do you good. Don't you dare take off."

As if she could. Her legs were leaden. Her chest so tight with grief, she could barely pull in a full breath. "Don't worry, I won't."

The cottage was bright blue trimmed with yellow, its wrought-iron fence lovingly tended, no different from the scant front garden. Flowers in every conceivable color crowded ferns, bushes and plants Gabe couldn't identify.

Although the humidity wasn't as bad today as it had been, he was already wilted, his shirt plastered to his damp back. The last time he'd sweated this much was in grade school when Sister Xavier had sent him to the principal's office for throwing spitballs at Desiree Tremaine, a girl he'd liked but hadn't gotten up the nerve to talk to. Romance had been so uncomplicated then. Now... He'd finally gotten enough courage to come here and didn't want to leave without doing what he had to.

He rapped harder.

"Coming. Be patient." The lock clacked and the door swung inward.

Iona Queen glanced up at him. She was in her mid-sixties, according to her driver's license, and still quite beautiful. A red turban hid her hair. Her gown matched the headdress. She wasn't as tall or curvy as Constance.

Gabe risked a smile. "Ms. Queen."

She stared at him, recognition in her eyes.

He didn't have to ask if Constance had talked about him. "Can I see your daughter, please?"

Iona pursed her lips. "What took you so long?" Sounds from a game show poured from another room. Despite the screeching contestants, she spoke quietly. "It's been nearly a week. Why'd you wait till now?"

Gabe hadn't expected her questions and didn't know what to say. Before coming here, he'd worried she'd throw him off her property and would call the cops, his colleagues actually, to keep him away. "I...ah..."

"Still not sure what you want?"

She certainly got straight to the point. "Actually, I am. Can I see Constance? Please."

Iona stepped aside but grabbed his sleeve before he got too deep into the cool, spotless house. "You hurt her before. Don't do it again."

"No, ma'am." He spoke as quietly as she had. "Believe me, I didn't mean to. I was confused."

"You're mortal. You'll have to get over that if you want my daughter."

He needed Constance more than air, food or water. Always had. It had simply taken him several days to stew over their relationship, to mull the pros and cons. The cons still outweighed everything else, but Gabe couldn't stand another moment without her. He needed Constance in his life whatever way she came, because it made her who she was. "I'll do my best."

Iona released him and gestured to the hall. "She's in the first room on the right."

Gabe warned himself not to race to her. He didn't want to alarm. Being a cop, he noticed details as he would at a crime scene—highly polished furniture, vases abounding on the tables. Some held flowers, others incense sticks. Pictures yellowed with age decorated the walls. Deeper into the house, creole spices wafted toward him. His mouth watered at the tempting aromas.

Smelling Constance again would be so much better.

He stopped at the first doorway on the right. Joy and tenderness flooded him.

Constance lounged on the sofa, her hair falling in soft waves around her gorgeous face. She wore a white gown edged with a flouncy type thing at the bottom, similar to a little girl's party dress. If they had a daughter, she'd probably clothe her that way.

The notion should have scared him spitless, but didn't. He wanted her.

She pretended to read a Reader's Digest condensed book.

Gabe smiled. "It's upside down."

Her gaze shot up and held his. Surprise, wonder, confusion and disquiet registered.

Not what he had hoped for, but then it wasn't as bad as he'd feared. "Hi."

She pushed off the sofa and smoothed her hair and gown.

"Don't." He lifted his hands. "You're perfect just as you are."

Her eyes grew wet and cautious. "What are you doing here?"

"I came for you, just as you are."

She covered her mouth.

He hoped she'd done so to stifle a happy cry rather than an oath. He should have come sooner. Hell, he shouldn't have left her apartment that morning, no matter what she'd said. If he'd stayed, they could have talked things out.

She stepped toward him and stopped. "Just as I am? You don't know anything about me."

"I know your last name isn't Chastain." He wagged his finger. "Nothing but the truth from now on. Deal?"

She backed away. Her legs hit the sofa. "Depends on what you want to know."

"Not what you think. Look, I've already had a chat with Becca and the others at the service. I know what they are—ah, who they are. Even saw the flames in Zoe's and Stefin's eyes. It was really something. I've never sweated so much in my life."

Constance frowned. "Becca showed you everything? She invited you to the service?"

"I went there on my own and more or less caught everyone off-guard."

She edged closer. "Were you looking for me?"

He was sorry he'd insisted on honesty between them. "No."

She halted. "Then why would you go there?"

"I thought maybe you had problems, like your blood sugar was too low or you were suffering from PTSD or—"

"Wait. You thought I had post-traumatic stress disorder?"

"It was all I could come up with to explain what you'd told me."

"Meaning you didn't believe me. And because you didn't, you went to my co-workers, *my friends*, to find out the truth."

He had and didn't regret that decision any longer. Someday he might feel the same about these moments. "Baby, I'm begging you to give me a break here. I'm mortal, okay? I don't get hit with this stuff on a daily basis. I needed some time to digest it."

Instead of softening, as he'd hoped, she stood even straighter. "Did you go to the service to demand my personnel records?"

"Absolutely not. I was going to ask everyone what they knew about you, but didn't have a chance." He lifted his shoulders. "Not after I saw what was going on."

"You believed me then and only then."

"I feel horrible for not having done so before, but like I said, I'm mortal." He prayed she'd cut him some slack.

Her mood remained cool. "You just found out today that I was telling you the truth? You came here directly from there?"

Gabe wished it were so. "I went there the same afternoon you told me to leave your place and not come back."

"And you waited until now to come by?" She made a face. "Becca's known for nearly a week and even she didn't bother to tell me?"

"You wouldn't talk to her," Iona spoke from the hall.

"Mama, please."

She stood in the doorway. "If you two want privacy, go outside and leave me to my TV program. It's a beautiful day. You should get some fresh air."

Gabe offered his hand to Constance, hoping she'd take it.

She merely stared, sending his hopes plunging. Once he lowered his hand, she crossed the room. "We can go out to the backyard."

Small and bricked in, the space boasted wrought-iron patio furniture and more plants. "Did you grow up here?" He was hungry to know everything about her.

She scowled at the back window.

Gabe guessed her mom was watching.

Constance turned to him. "Yeah, I did grow up here, just Mama and me. Forget what I told you about my parents. It was all lies. I never knew my dad. I'm not even sure who he is, though I'm thinking Morgan Freeman or Colin Powell. My mom came across both guys in the past. Interesting stories. By the way, she's also a voodoo priestess, a legend in our community. In time, I hope to be too, because it's my life's calling, my special talent, what I do for a living and always will. No. Matter. What."

She was trying to run him away or test him. Gabe was too tired and lonely to play games. "She seems like a fine woman. I hope someday she'll like me."

"She finally moved away from the window, so my guess is she trusts you. That's a big deal, since she isn't remotely the same as you. Neither am I. As you've said repeatedly today, you're mortal."

He took her hand and squeezed it gently. "Forgive me for that. As far as I'm concerned, I don't care that we're different. I'm glad we are. Makes things interesting."

"You say that now."

"I should have said it the moment I knew the truth. I'll never forgive myself for not doing so."

She searched his face. Desire softened her features.

He couldn't have been happier. "We good?"

Her tenderness faded. She grew distant again and eased her hand from his. "You waited nearly a week before trying to see me. No, we're not good. You disappeared after we talked. Or rather, I talked and you refused to listen. Why didn't you come back that first day?"

"You told me not to."

"And you used it as an excuse? You didn't call, either. Did I say anything about you not phoning me? You went to the service to find out about my so-called problem, and once you knew everything, you stayed away, but now you're suddenly here?"

"It wasn't sudden." He captured her hand and held it between his. "I never stopped thinking of us. I won't lie—all of this scares the shit out of me. It's so foreign to everything I've ever known. But I'm willing to give it a try and see where our feelings take us, if you want to."

"Why?"

"Because I'm falling for you, have been since the beginning, and I hope you're doing the same with me."

She regarded him intently. "You mean it?"

"Would I be here sweating bullets if I didn't?"

Constance smiled but killed it quickly. "I love everyone at the service and I won't have anyone saying they're creatures or monsters or whatever the pejorative happens to be."

"I haven't and I won't. It's not the kind of man I am. I know what it's like not to belong. Hopefully, your friends will become mine, too, and we can make life easier on each other."

"Easier?" She screwed up her mouth. "The guys are demons and a former satyr who wouldn't know how to act in polite company if you gave them detailed instructions. Then there's a nervous fairy, a nympho genie and a half-ass witch. Believe me, this won't be easy."

"That's perfectly all right, especially when it comes to the women. They're always trouble when you get right down to it. But the guys and I will be there to keep you ladies in line."

"What?" She smacked his pec.

Laughing, he pulled her close and hugged her as hard as he dared. He surrendered to emotion he'd held back too damn long. "God, I've missed you, baby." He buried his face in her hair.

Constance sagged against him. "I'm still pissed." She embraced him as tightly as he did her. "You really hurt me."

"I didn't mean to. I was surprised, confused and totally stupid. I swear, it won't happen again."

She snuggled closer. "Tell me how much you missed me. Could you sleep?"

"Fuck no. I'm dead on my feet right now."

"How about eating? Were you able to?"

"I haven't swallowed anything except coffee, vitamins, fruit drinks, milk and lots of beer."

"Lucky you, I haven't had anything stronger than tea. Have you cried?"

He went hot from embarrassment and was about to blow off her question with a smart-ass comment but thought better of it. He loosened his hold and eased back. "When I thought I'd never see you again because you were finished with me for good, yeah, I did cry. Only once though. Okay, twice. But don't you dare tell anyone. It's our secret, and your mom's, if she's listening."

Constance laughed softly. "My lips are sealed."

"They better not be." He covered her mouth with his and thrust his tongue inside.

She welcomed his passion and stoked it with her own.

The back door opened and closed just as quickly.

Neither bothered looking over at her mother's quick retreat.

He and Constance kissed as though starved for closeness, which they were. They'd always been outcasts, searching for a place to belong in a hostile, unforgiving world.

As far as Gabe was concerned, they didn't have to look any further. They had each other now. They'd build from there.

Epilogue

Three months later...

The early October evening was balmy, dusk not having yet tamed today's heat. It was beautiful though and romantic too, the faint crescent moon surrounded by countless stars. A good thing for the weres and vamps who were still going through their makeovers. The growing darkness allowed them to participate in this evening's celebration — Constance's fifth anniversary at the service.

As guest of honor, she wore a tall tiara, courtesy of MJ, and held a fairy wand, thanks to Heather.

Earlier, Heather had confessed the truth. "I got it on eBay. Don't worry about breaking it or anything. It's not real."

Constance had fought laughter at Heather's sweet naiveté. She'd rip out her tongue before hurting her or anyone here. They were simply too precious, especially Gabe.

He'd outdone himself with this surprise bash, even renting a New Orleans's steamboat for a private dinner cruise. Across the water, city lights sparkled like jewels, the bright colors bleeding into the mighty Mississippi. In here, a band played while everyone danced or enjoyed a feast that included pork loin, southern fried fish, rib roast, creole spinach, sweet potatoes and freshly baked bread.

Mouthwatering scents filled the air but didn't impress the vamps who had yet to suppress their beasts. They wanted something more, and Gabe had provided it.

Constance wasn't certain how he'd smuggled bottles of blood on board. He'd even supplied the imported stuff Becca offered at the service. Several vamps lifted their drinks to acknowledge what he'd done. Others patted his back or had shaken his hand in thanks.

Unlike the evening at Rambeau's, when Quentin had unnerved him, Gabe was one of the gang now, accepting everyone for who or what they were.

They liked him, too.

Constance's feelings had blossomed into such boundless love she seemed ready to burst at times. Weeks ago, she'd confessed her feelings to Gabe, and he'd done the same to her. They'd grinned like fools rather than freaking out.

They were building a life together, a home. Something Constance had never believed she'd have.

She turned to him.

Stefin stepped between their chairs. "Detective Legrand—Gabe."

Constance tapped Stefin to get his attention.

He edged away and looked at her.

"Seriously, it's just Gabe." She must have told Stefin so a thousand times.

He lifted his chin, his mood imperious. "I know, but his full name sounds more impressive. Like a detective who can get things done." He spoke to Gabe. "The guys and I need your help with a problem we have."

Constance sensed what it might be.

Anatol, Daemon and Taro huddled together near the last table, beer bottles in hand. Rather than watch MJ and Heather shaking their booties on the dance floor, they stared at Wynona, the newest enforcer. She also happened to be a reaper. Tall and slender, except for her impressive rack, she was quite beautiful, her long white hair complementing a snowy complexion and silver eyes.

Despite Wynona's great looks, no one at the table spoke to her. They'd scooted their chairs far away, leaving her in emptiness.

Constance felt bad about that.

Taro, Daemon and Anatol glared at Wynona. She scowled at them.

A defensive response. Constance sensed Wynona was as lonely as she'd once been, feeling as unwanted. The only mortals Wynona met were those she was going to haul from this planet into the Great Unknown. Not a good way to meet guys or build a lasting relationship. The clients had little use for her, given they were already on the other side, literally or physically. Besides, they'd come to the service so they could spruce up for mortal babes, not someone like her.

Gabe looked at Stefin. "What's the problem you guys have?"

"The reaper, what else? She's a nuisance, but I've figured a way to fix it." He rocked on his heels. "While you distract her with your badge and gun, the guys and I will tie her up. The rope on deck will work fine. Once we chain something heavy to her feet, maybe the anchor, we can throw her overboard and watch her sink to the bottom of the river where she belongs. No one will ever know."

"I don't think so." Constance pressed her cheek to Gabe's so Stefin couldn't overhear. "Better have a talk with them right now before they do something loony. If all else fails, cuff them to the chairs."

"I'd rather do that to you."

She squeezed his thigh. "Later, in bed."

"Sounds good. With them, though, a little steel isn't much of a deterrent against their powers. Why don't they use their supernatural stuff against hers?"

"A reaper's are stronger. The only way they can do what they want is to outwit her first. Just like you'll get them to back off by saying your cuffs have magical powers."

"Seriously?"

"Hey, they've always made me surrender."

He sniggered. "Thanks, but I doubt they'll be impressed. How about we get Zoe to keep them in line? Her job after all." He glanced around. "Where is she?"

Constance pointed.

Zoe was across the room, wedged between a vamp and a were who growled and hissed at each other. Their mortal dates looked on, faces enthralled at them rumbling. A warlock, who'd just finished his makeover, collected cash from the gathering crowd. Bets on who'd win the fight.

Before anything went down, Zoe dug her spike heel into the vamp's foot and rammed her elbow into the were's gut. They doubled over in pain. As she lectured them, smoke poured from her hair.

Constance stated the obvious. "Zoe has her hands full right now."

"What about your boss?" Gabe leaned back and craned his neck.

Across the room, Becca and Eric offered each other food and shared a kiss, oblivious to everything and everyone except each other.

Constance bumped Gabe's arm. "Also busy."

Stefin huffed. "You're not listening to me."

"Sorry." She gave him her full attention, praying it would last before she got bored and drifted. "What were you saying?"

"I was speaking to him." He gripped Gabe's shoulder and brightened. "I have an even better plan than the last one Constance didn't like." He gave her a pissy stare then spoke to Gabe. "I saw a storage area on the way here. After we catch the reaper unaware and tie her up, we can put her in one of those units. As long as we pay the monthly fee, no one will ever find her."

Constance slapped Stefin's arm. "Her name is Wynona. And, no, don't even think of doing what you said or anything else when it comes to her." She shot Gabe a look. "Better go. Please."

He lifted a finger to Stefin. "Don't move. I'll be with you in a sec."

"Why not now?"

"Because of this." Gabe cradled Constance's face and kissed her indecently deep and long, leaving her breathless.

She sucked in air.

He settled his mouth on her ear. "Stefin and the others are just jealous of Wynona invading their territory. This is nothing more than talk. Trust me cops are the same when a woman's hired. The guys will eventually chill like you said Zoe did once she no longer felt threatened by The Unholy Trio."

"Sweetie, she calmed down after unleashing her powers on Stefin and fucking up the office. Do you really want a battle of the titans here tonight with it reported on the front page of *The Times-Picayune*?"

"Guess I better take care of this." He kissed her longingly and followed Stefin to the others.

They spoke. Daemon mellowed fast, along with the rest. Stefin alone resisted, puffing out his chest and gesturing dramatically. Cool as could be, Gabe said something to deflate him.

Damn, he was amazing. Despite Stefin's supernatural powers and his sulfur stench, he didn't intimidate Gabe in the least. Nothing did, except the thought of losing her.

That wasn't going to happen.

Flushed with love and confidence, Constance enjoyed the festivities, sipping her wine, chowing down and slow dancing with her man. He, Daemon, Taro and Anatol lifted her in a chair above their shoulders.

She shrieked and laughed.

They paraded her around the room as if she were the newly crowned queen.

Guests got into the act. The guys bowed dutifully to her and the women curtsied. Some kissed her many rings.

A subtle pop sounded. Confetti filled everyone's hands, courtesy of MJ. The band was so busy playing, they didn't notice the magic. The supernaturals tossed the brightly colored pieces at Constance.

She giggled. "Enough! I haven't even gotten a raise yet."

The crowd quieted, their attention falling on Becca. She'd just finished sucking Eric's neck and left a huge hickey. When she noticed everyone staring at her, she turned fifty shades of red. "What?"

"Constance was asking about her raise." Zoe crossed her arms. "When does she get it?"

Becca smiled at Constance. "It'll be in your next paycheck, as you well know."

An approving roar filled the room.

Afterward, all hell broke loose in a good way. Mortals and immortals danced, snuggled, kissed, ate, talked and laughed.

Gabe spirited Constance to the deck. The cool air felt heavenly against her moist skin. She was about to adjust her crown when he stopped her.

"Don't. You're perfect as you are." He regarded her for a long moment.

She smiled self-consciously. "What?"

"Thank you for opening my eyes."

"To how perfect I am and always will be?"

His shoulders shook with his quiet laughter. "That, too, except for your swelled head. I meant showing me how good these folks are, and how they've always walked among people like me."

"Are you saying you've noticed more?"

"Couple on the force, I think."

"Oh my God." That was better than she could have hoped for. "Now you'll have someone to talk to there too."

"If they are what I'm thinking. Right now, I'm leaning toward warlocks. Could be they're simply pricks of the mortal variety."

"Whenever you're sure, invite them into the group. The more the merrier. Hey, maybe one of them will like Wynona."

"Maybe." Gabe pressed against her. Naked desire filled his gorgeous eyes. "Right now, I'd prefer to concentrate on you. No one else."

The band played *Like I'm Gonna Lose You*. A sweet-sad song that oddly enough filled Constance with hope. She'd do all she could and then some to make certain her and Gabe's romance not only lasted but flourished.

As the rest of the crowd partied, Gabe kissed her, his unrestrained love enhanced by tenderness, respect and a shitload of lust.

The holy trifecta.

Precisely what Constance had always needed and would enjoy for the rest of their days.

Want to see more from this author? Here's a taster for you to enjoy!

Taming the Beast: Disciplining the Beast
Tina Donahue

Excerpt

Wynona lifted her face and sniffed.

A vulnerable soul. Its fragrance was a mixture that combined fragile life, everlasting death, sweet innocence and decadent sin—each an aphrodisiac to a reaper.

She gripped her desk to stay put rather than snatching the lovely spirit. She'd been a bad girl in the past, stealing souls without authorization, and was paying big time for that now. The powers that be had banished her to this godforsaken place—From Crud to Stud, a New Orleans makeover service for supernatural beings.

Weres howled, vamps hissed, zombies moaned.

The scent beckoned once more, tempting her beyond restraint. She gritted her teeth and tried to focus on her stupid paperwork. Her concentration and resolve wavered. Maybe if she simply looked at the potential victim but didn't touch, everything would be all right.

She stalked down the hall.

A female staff member ground to a quick halt, pivoted and hurried into a treatment room. Other doors closed before Wynona could pass, telling her what she'd already known. No one liked reapers, not even otherworldly beings who didn't have souls to lose. Given that she couldn't hurt them as she would a mortal, they could have at least tried to be cordial and said "Hi" or shot the breeze. Made her feel like a team member rather than a pariah.

Another door closed. More than a few staffers inside threw the locks.

Ignoring their snubs, she focused on Heather, the receptionist. Her blindingly white dress matched her pale hair and skin. As a good fairy, she healed those in pain and radiated kindness needed by the lonely. Her soul was pure as a baby's first breath and off-limits.

Rather than look at her computer, Heather smiled sweetly at someone Wynona couldn't see.

She drew closer. At her approach, the lights flickered from the vibes she gave off. She likened it to an early warning system that let mortals and supernaturals know she was in the area and they had better watch out. As if she didn't already have enough problems snatching souls. This she didn't need.

Heather lifted her face to the pulsing lights then looked at the hall.

Wynona arched one eyebrow in greeting.

Rather than offer a nod, grin or a "Hey, how you doing?" in return, Heather's lovely face grew even ashier. She fumbled in her desk drawer, yanked out a crucifix and held it up like actors did in those old Dracula movies. Her hands shook. "I'm sorry. This is rude, I know, but— I'm sorry."

Wynona wasn't certain whether to laugh at Heather's apologetic nature, groan at being treated so lousily or surrender to the status quo and skulk back to her office to hide out until someone needed her. The soul fragrance swirled near, pulling her closer. "No offense taken."

"Please stay where you are."

She couldn't and picked up speed.

Constance rounded the corner.

Wynona reared back.

So did Constance. Her silky gown swished around her ample curves, the hot-pink color complementing her ebony complexion. She took in Wynona then Heather.

"Put that down." Constance jabbed her thumb at the cross. "That's for vamps, not reapers, unless you want to whack her on the head to get her to back off."

Wynona lifted her chin. "From doing what? I was merely walking down the hall."

"Uh-huh." Constance gave her a knowing look. "Say the word and I can make you forget everything you were about to do."

Big talk. However, Constance was a damn good voodoo priestess with a talent for removing memories. Once her bejeweled fingers touched anyone's skull, poof, the past was history. "How about you touch me and I touch you in return?"

"Wynona." Heather's cheeks pinked up. "You shouldn't talk like that."

Strange advice from a good fairy who has a thing going with a lusty former satyr and counts a nympho genie as her BFF. "I wasn't taking about sex, hon."

Heather went into a full-body blush.

Constance huffed. "No reaping here, got it? Especially staff members' souls."

"Yes, ma'am. But how about ones from clients who are still alive?" She itched to get past her to the source emitting the delicious fragrance. From where she stood, she still couldn't see everything in the reception area.

Feathery ferns and potted plants overran the cozy space, making it a veritable forest. Faux gas fixtures graced the coral walls. Coming in here was like stepping back in time, the dated, romantic feel a cover for what really went on. Moonlight therapy for weres. Treatments to tame bloodsucking vamps. Speech and personality programs for zombies. Potions for every purpose so supernatural beings could move among the unsuspecting and get it on with mortal babes.

Constance squared her shoulders. "We don't bite the hands that feed us. Behave yourself and get back to work."

"Wait." Heather stood. "There's someone here to see you, Wynona."

Hmm. No one ever willingly approached her except another reaper who had nothing to lose. Just once, she'd like to browbeat a shifter into a treatment room and take out her frustration on him rather than her own kind. "Who wants to see me? Or rather, what?"

Heather bit her lower lip.

A sure sign another reaper awaited. Possibly one she'd dated only to have him dump her so he could tame his beast here and give a mortal woman his best. Just what she didn't need, another louse. She drooped.

Unfortunately, her disappointment didn't change things. She'd been put here as an enforcer to get the clients where they should be and strap them in or subdue them so other staff members could work their magic. If a vamp, zombie or reaper got out of line or too frisky during treatment, it was her sworn duty to make them behave. If she didn't, there would be hell to pay. Literally. She passed Constance but didn't get far. Her legs refused to work.

The guy on the sofa pushed to his feet.

His scent washed over her, snatching her breath. If goodness and starshine had an odor, that would be his, the fragrance of an unsullied soul. Definitely not a reaper. Not a mortal, either.

That reality should have had her bolting down the hall before she did something bad.

His outstanding looks kept her rooted to the spot. He was a large man, six-three or more, with shoulders that went from here to tomorrow. His broad chest, flat belly and powerful thighs were the stuff of Greek myths wrapped in fashionable duds straight from *GQ*— charcoal-colored pants and a midnight-blue shirt. Both garments draped his form beautifully, including the impressive bulge behind his fly.

Apollo had nothing on this dude.

As far as she could tell, he was hung better than most gods and mortals. In human years, he was likely early to mid-thirties. He'd tied back his long raven hair, though a few silky strands had escaped to graze his forehead and firm jaw.

Her knees went watery.

Dark stubble dusted his cheeks, chin and upper lip. His complexion was a healthy bronze, eyes lushly lashed, their color a deeper blue than sapphires, his gaze deliciously intense.

Give him cuffs and a whip along with free rein and he'd rock a BDSM chamber any day.

Her insides went gooey.

Of course, the goodness rolling off him was a problem. He couldn't be here for a makeover. There was nowhere to go from perfect, unless…

He might want to release his beast, the same as Eric had done a few years back. As a direct descendant of Cupid, Eric had wanted to ditch his courtly demeanor and become a bad boy to snag the babes. After he'd met

Becca, the half-witch who owned this joint, he'd changed his mind about other women and hooked up with her for life.

A sweet dream Wynona coveted but didn't expect for herself. However, if this guy wanted someone to corrupt him and had heard about her hardcore ways, how could she say no?

She sashayed across the room and stopped close enough for them to kiss. He didn't back up or take off. She liked that. Gave her a chance to indulge.

His full mouth had probably fueled countless female wet dreams, the cleft in his chin was beyond lickable and the interest in his gaze was the best of all. He searched her eyes the way a mortal did when wanting to touch another person's soul.

If she'd had one, she wouldn't have let him look inside. Being defenseless led to more sorrow and hurt. *No, thank you.* She'd had an eternity dealing with that crap. "Hey there, I'm Wynona."

She would have offered to shake his hand, but one touch from a reaper and anyone alive was toast, except for select supernatural beings. As a rule, those whose powers were equal to or greater than hers. She wanted to ask him what he was but waited, hoping skin-to-skin contact wouldn't be verboten for them.

"Wynona." He inclined his head. A lock fell past his ear and skimmed his cheek.

Her mouth watered.

"I'm Rafael."

Indeed, he was. A killer name for a sexy man. "And what brings you here tonight, Rafael?"

"You."

He couldn't have given a better answer. Her spirits soared. "So, you've heard of me, huh?"

"Repeatedly and at length." His cheeks darkened.

She flushed with excitement too. "What kind of makeover did you want?"

"I don't. That is, none." He glanced past her to Heather and Constance.

Heather pretended to work rather than eavesdrop. Constance didn't budge, all eyes and ears. Stefin, a demon enforcer, had joined her.

He and the other male enforcement team had given Wynona a fucking hard time from the second she'd started at this place. She glared at him.

He glowered right back, the flames in his eyes blazing.

She spoke to Rafael. "None? You mean, as in, no taming your beast? So, you're here to free your wayward urges, right?"

His forehead turned red but desire flashed in his eyes. "No. I need to rein yours in."

Her hope spiked a thousand percent. "You're into BDSM too?" She smiled slyly. "You like being a Master?"

Heather made a strangled noise.

Constance offered a throaty moan that sounded beyond turned on.

Rafael had stopped breathing seconds ago. He pulled in some air. "I'm your parole officer."

Wynona went colder than a vamp then hotter than a menopausal woman. "What? Wait. I know what my parole officer looks like. Little dude with a face only a blind mother could love and a personality on par with overcooked spaghetti." Her gesture took in Rafael's magnificence. "Definitely not you."

"Hold it." Stefin strode to them, his long blond hair bobbing with each step. "She was in prison, like me?"

During his mortal days, he'd been in the Russian mafia, which had landed him a front seat in Hell.

Rafael wrinkled his nose. Heather sprayed her baby powder scent. The fragrance did little to eliminate the sulfur stench exuded by Stefin and all demons.

Rafael backed away from him. "We're trying to avoid prison for Wynona. The group sent me here to make certain she behaves."

Stefin nodded. "What group is that?"

"Supernatural Authority in Charge of Souls, what else?" Wynona curled her upper lip at him. "SACS for short. They suck, just like you do." She faced Rafael. "What happened to the other guy?"

"Got kicked upstairs."

"Because he made my existence miserable?"

Stefin wedged himself between her and Rafael. "Tell me how to get rid of her...Wynona." He made a gagging sound from speaking her name for once. "I'll do it for free. I could even pay you for the information. We have leather restraints here, manacles for the problem cases—rope, too. Whatever we need. There are countless storage facilities around. We can tie her up and dump her in one of them. As long as we pay the fee, no one will ever know she's there."

Constance cleared her throat. "Wynona would."

Stefin waved dismissively.

Heather tried to frown, not an easy thing for a good fairy. "No one should hurt her or anyone else. Maybe you guys should talk in her office where it's private."

"Good idea." Stefin pivoted and gestured to lead the way.

Constance grabbed his arm. "Not you, Wynona and Rafael. Go on." She flicked her hand at them. "We'll give you guys all the time you need."

Now, she wants to be friendly.

Wynona tramped down the hall, teeth bared. A were halted just outside a treatment room, spotted her and ducked back inside.

She would have followed and locked Rafael out if it would have done her any good.

Of all the rotten luck. She'd just gotten her last guy to back off and now she had a new one to break in or break. Whatever it took. Even if Rafael smelled better than a squeaky-clean soul and was hotter than a romance cover model, he was still the enemy.

She stopped at her office and gestured him inside.

He backed into the snug space, gaze boring into hers—a warning not to pull anything.

Commanding and hot. The whole enchilada.

She trembled in delight and hated herself for it.

Home of Erotic Romance

Sign up for our newsletter and find out about all our
romance book releases, eBook sales and promotions,
sneak peeks and FREE romance books!

About the Author

Tina is an Amazon and international bestselling novelist who writes passionate romance for every taste–'heat with heart'–for traditional publishers and indie. Booklist, Publisher's Weekly, Romantic Times and numerous online sites have praised her work. She's won Readers' Choice Awards, was named a finalist in the EPIC competition, received a Book of the Year award, The Golden Nib Award, awards of merit in the RWA Holt Medallion competitions, and second place in the NEC RWA contests. She's featured in the Novel & Short Story Writer's Market. Before penning romances, she worked at a major Hollywood production company in Story Direction.

Tina loves to hear from readers. You can find her contact information, website details and author profile page at https://www.totallybound.com